Franklin Pierce Sever

The Progressive Speller

a complete spelling book

Franklin Pierce Sever

The Progressive Speller
a complete spelling book

ISBN/EAN: 9783337400828

Printed in Europe, USA, Canada, Australia, Japan

Cover: Foto ©Andreas Hilbeck / pixelio.de

More available books at **www.hansebooks.com**

THE

PROGRESSIVE SPELLER

A COMPLETE SPELLING BOOK

ARRANGED FOR

ADVANCED PRIMARY, INTERMEDIATE,
AND GRAMMAR GRADES

F. P. SEVER

BOSTON, U.S.A.

D. C. HEATH & CO., PUBLISHERS

1893

PREFACE.

THE object in preparing this book is to meet the require-
ments of a progressive age, which calls for something more
in spelling than the mere conning of columns of words, isolated
from language, and too frequently without meaning or interest
to the learner.

The following are among the principles observed and the
features made prominent: —

1. Reasonable time and space are given to the meaning
and use of words in connection with their spelling.

2. Since we speak English more than we write it, correct
pronunciation is given place in proportion to its importance,
though all marks and dots are valueless unless their signifi-
cance is learned and carefully applied in every-day practice.

3. Effort is made to render the work attractive as well
as useful to the learner by the introduction of letter-writing;
by word and sentence building; by giving variety in arrangement; and by conforming, in subject-matter, to the capacity
of the average child and the natural order of mind growth.

4. The "seat work" involved throughout the book is more
than copy work, — it implies "work with words." It is designed

as practice to promote facility in expression and accuracy in the use of English.

5. Homonyms, synonyms, and antonyms are given the attention and prominence that their importance demands.

6. The etymological and dictionary work is conveniently arranged, is sufficiently suggestive, and will furnish a basis for more extended study of language.

7. Script is introduced as a guide to the younger pupils in written work, and to give the appearance of words in that form.

8. Part I. is peculiarly adapted to oral work in class. In Part II. ample provision is made for constructive work (in writing, if so preferred) by the more advanced pupils during "study hour."

9. The gradation of work is not based on any "time" graded school, but is on the easy and natural order known to be in harmony with *all* mind power and mind growth.

10. Finally, — if the ideas of the author are correct, — the teacher's duty does not end with "giving out" the words; the student can do more than memorize perplexing combinations of letters; teacher and pupil can join in a most delightful employment, — the study of the spelling of words and the ideas they represent; expressing new thoughts by varying the relations of the component parts, and converting the tedious hour of the "spelling class" into a pleasant ramble in the fields and byways of our language.

F. P. S.

PART I.

THE PROGRESSIVE SPELLER.

ā *long (– macron)*   ă *short (⌣ breve)*

1. dāy	āte	hăd	lăp
2. ray	age	lad	cap
3. play	ape	mad	map
4. hay	bay	pad	tap
5. way	lay	sad	sap

ē *long*   ĕ *short*

' 6. tēa	hē	mĕt	hĕn
7. key	me	pet	ten
8. sea	be	let	men
9. see	bee	set	pen
10. eat	tree	get	den

1

ī *long*		ĭ *short*	
1. īce	nīce	pĭn	ĭt
2. ivy	price	fin	bit
3. time	dice	tin	fit
4. pile	rice	win	sit
5. pike	twice	sin	wit

ō *long*		ŏ *short*	
6. fōe	gō	gŏt	lŏg
7. toe	so	rot	hog
8. tow	no	not	fog
9. row	ho	pot	dog
10. roe	hoe	hot	Tom

ū *long*		ŭ *short*	
11. tūne	lūte	bŭd	cŭb
12. mule	cube	mud	cup
13. cute	tube	fun	sup
14. mute	nude	run	gun
15. use	sued	sun	nut

ȳ *long*		*long*	*short*
1. flȳ	sly	pāge	slăp
2. try	wry	lēaf	lŏft
3. pry	sky	fîre	sĭft
4. cry	type	sōre	trŏt
5. dry	defy	denȳ	cŭp

ä, *Italian, as in* ärm

6. ärm	*arm*	härp	*harp*
7. far	*far*	farm	*farm*
8. jar	*jar*	lark	*lark*
9. art	*art*	park	*park*
10. tar	*tar*	car	*car*

ạ, *broad, as in* ạll

11. ạll	*all*	chạlk	*chalk*
12. tall	*tall*	walk	*walk*
13. call	*call*	talk	*talk*
14. ball	*ball*	draw	*draw*
15. salt	*salt*	drawn	*drawn*

â, *caret, as in* âir

1. âir	*air*	glâre	*glare*
2. hair	*hair*	hare	*hare*
3. fair	*fair*	fare	*fare*
4. chair	*chair*	rare	*rare*
5. lair	*lair*	share	*share*

a̧ *and* ȧ

6. wa̧tch	*watch*	ga̓sp	*gasp*
7. wad	*wad*	pass	*pass*
8. wander	*wander*	ask	*ask*
9. wasp	*wasp*	fast	*fast*
10. wash	*wash*	chant	*chant*

Seven sounds of a. (*Review*)

ā	ă	ä	a̧
11. spāde	băt	fäther	broa̧d
12. grade	flat	harm	halter
13. trade	gnat	harvest	water
14. tame	glad	half	war
15. lame	sapling	calf	dwarf

â	ạ	à	
1. snâre	wạs	màss	slāte
2. pare	walrus	master	ăpple
3. fair	wallop	mastiff	yärd
4. pear	wallow	plaster	wạll
5. beware	walnut	last	ângle

ê *like* â   ᶒ *like* ā

6. whêre	*where*	they	*they*
7. there	*there*	whey	*whey*
8. ere	*ere*	obey	*obey*
9. ne'er	*ne'er*	eight	*eight*
10. heir	*heir*	weight	*weight*

ĕ *before* **r**, *as in verge*

11. vĕrge	*verge*	ĕrr	*err*
12. prefẽr	*prefer*	earth	*earth*
13. defer	*defer*	heard	*heard*
14. mercy	*mercy*	herd	*herd*
15. term	*term*	serve	*serve*

Five sounds of e. (Review)

c̄	ĕ	ê *like* â	ẽ
1. hēat	whet	whêrc	sĕrvant
2. seat	beset	wherefore	verdant
3. cheat	cadet	e *like* ā	refer
4. each	beget	neighbor	fertile

ï *and* ĭ

ï *like* ē		ĭ *like* ĕ	
5. machïne	*machine*	fĭrst	*first*
6. marine	*marine*	third	*third*
7. morphine	*morphine*	firm	*firm*
8. routine	*routine*	virgin	*virgin*

ô *and* ȯ

ô *like* a		ȯ *like* ŭ	
9. fôrm	*form*	dȯve	*dove*
10. storm	*storm*	love	*love*
11. order	*order*	other	*other*
12. stork	*stork*	done	*done*

ǫ *and* ọ .

ǫ *like* ōō   ọ *like* ŏŏ

1. mǫve	*move*	wọlf	*wolf*
2. prove	*prove*	woman	*woman*
3. do	*do*	would	*would*
4. you	*you*	could	*could*

ōō *and* oo

ōō *long*   ŏŏ *short*

5. mōōn	*moon*	bŏŏk	*book*
6. soon	*soon*	look	*look*
7. spoon	*spoon*	hook	*hook*
8. bloom	*bloom*	took	*took*

ṳ, û, *and* ụ

              û *before* r.

9. rṳde	*rude*	ûrge	*urge*
10. rule	*rule*	purge	*purge*
		ụ *like* ŏŏ	
11. prune	*prune*	pụll	*pull*
12. cruel	*cruel*	full	*full*

Diphthongs oi, oy, ow

oi	oy	ou	ow
1. oil	toy	out	owl
2. boil	joy	scout	howl
3. coil	boy	shout	growl
4. toil	troy	trout	powder
5. broil	oyster	ground	prow

b, c, d

b	ç soft	e hard	d
6. bug	çedar	erown	dish
7. black	cider	cot	drive
8. brick	certain	clot	drink
9. bucket	city	colt	damp
10. basket	cypress	clown	dark

f, g, h

f	ḡ hard	ġ soft	h
11. flog	ḡlade	ġem	hum
12. fife	glee	gentry	harm
13. fifty	grind	gibbet	happy
14. first	glad	germ	hornet
15. fight	gallop	gist	hurry

j, k, l, m

j	k	l	m
1 jump	king	lamp	musket
2. jay	keep	lazy	many
3. junk	kind	lofty	muslin
4. jolly	kitchen	line	mason
5. jelly	kick	limp	mitten

n, p, q

n	n̠	p	q
6. name	link	prince	queen
7. navy	linger	prose	quickly
8. night	bethink	power	quail
9. near	longer	pretty	quill
10. noise	uncle	plant	quality

r, s, t

r	s sharp	s̠ soft	t
11. roast	soft	amus̠e	tone
12. rainbow	same	disease	note
13. rafter	smile	dismal	moist
14. rest	silly	dissolve	honest
15. rival	soap	disown	must

v, x, z

v	x sharp	x̱ soft	z
1. voice	explain	example	zone
2. violet	except	exempt	zebra
3. vulture	extend	exist	frozen
4. vinegar	exclaim	exhaust	size
5. vase	exclude	exhort	buzz

w	y
wool	yeast
wet	young
waist	your
wait	yard
welcome	yonder

Lesson 1.

The children are all at school. The sun is high in the sky. Do not go to sleep yet. We will now spell for our teacher. She likes to hear us spell

Rule 1. — *Every sentence should begin with a capital letter.*

all	äre	ăt	hīgh	ĭn
spĕll	slēēp	yĕt	tēacher	ŭp

Lesson 2.

căn	*can*	sĭng	*sing*
mīce	*mice*	jŭmp	*jump*
līke	*like*	cătch	*catch*
bīrd	*bird*	kĭtten	*kitten*
sēēds	*seeds*	sĭnger	*singer*

To the Teacher. — Require the pupil to use these words in original sentences.

Lesson 3.

FOR COPY AND DICTATION.

The lambs are very gay. They make nice pets. Most lambs are white. Some rabbits are white. Which would you like best, a pet lamb or a pet rabbit?

Rule 2. — *End each question (sentence) with a question mark.*

gāy	lămbs	māke	nīce	răbbit
mōst	whīte	few	ạlso	līke

Lesson 4.

līve	*live*	wŏrkers	*workers*
hīve	*hive*	hŏney	*honey*
hăve	*have*	wạsp	*wasp*
shärp	*sharp*	wĭngs	*wings*
stĭngs	*stings*	greāt	*great*

To the Teacher. — Require the pupil to use these words in original sentences.

Lesson 5.

whạt	*what*	dọ	*do*
thăt	*that*	dȯes	*does*
māde	*made*	fôr	*for*
blīnd	*blind*	quĕstion	*question*
câre	*care*	wĭth	*with*

(See Note to Teacher, Lesson 4.)

Lesson 6.

Who made the stars? What makes them twinkle so? Could you go up to where they are in one hour? in one day? in one week? Could a little bird fly there? Will you tell us about the moon and stars?

stärs	twĭnkle	whêre	wĭll	hour
lĭttle	tĕll	about	mōōn	mākes

Lesson 7.

All fish are good swimmers. Do you know what some young fish are called? They are called minnows. Do you think a minnow would make a nice pet? Name five kinds of fish.

fish swimmers called know is kinds minnows think good name

Lesson 8.

NAMES OF OBJECTS IN THE SCHOOL-ROOM.

Note to Teacher. — Some of these words will serve as subjects for oral instruction in form, capacity, material, etc.

stōve	*stove*	măps	*maps*
châir	*chair*	chärts	*charts*
bĕll	*bell*	pointers	*pointers*
dĕsk	*desk*	erāsers	*erasers*
măp	*map*	slātes	*slates*

Lesson 9.

The farmer takes his grain to market. Here comes one now with a load of wheat. He drives a fine team of horses. They are noble animals. He treats them kindly.

farmer market grain takes noble kindly comes horses wheat treats

Lesson 10. — Review.

hĭgh	māde	nīce	greāt
tēacher	quĕstion	līke	wórkers
cătch	twĭnkle	yĕt	thăt
kĭtten	about	bĭrd	blīnd
mīce	mĭnnow	ŭp	why
mōst	whēat	sĭng	stärs
few	cómes	jŭmp	whêre
lămbs	cạlled	slēep	thĭnk
shärp	nōble	ạlso	knōw
hóney	câre	wạsp	fĭsh

Lesson 11.

Here comes Frank with his pet squirrel. He is a very happy boy. His elder brother, whose name is Henry, was in the woods one day He found a nest of young squirrels and brought Frank one for a pet.

Rule 3.—*Begin each proper name with a capital letter.*

Frank	Henry	squĭrrel	found	brother
brought	wŏŏds	elder	nĕst	whọse

Lesson 12.

Mary has named her doll. What do you think she calls it? She has named it Queen. Fannie calls her doll Bessie. Two girls and two dolls. Two and two are four.

Mary Fannie Queen Bessie named two doll four

(See Rule 3, above.)

Lesson 13.

Whose sled is this? Is it yours, Harry? What a nice one it is! Do you enjoy coasting? I think it fine sport to go down hill on a new sled. I like to skate on the pond when the ice is smooth.

slĕd	thĭs	cōasting	fīne	pŏnd
spōrt	quĕstion	märk	yọur	spōrt

Lesson 14.

ĕver	*ever*	flĕsh	*flesh*
färmer	*farmer*	shēar	*shear*
shēēp	*sheep*	mŭtton	*mutton*
May	*May*	măn	*man*
June	*June*	pōrk	*pork*

(See note, Lesson 2.)

Lesson 15.

James, if you will come with me, I will show you a pretty sight. Oh! one, two, three, four little eggs! How delicate they are! Do you think they will hatch?

Rule 4. — *Use an exclamation point after an exclaiming sentence.*

James	*James*	hătch	*hatch*
shōw	*show*	ĕxclamātion	*exclamation*
thrēē	*three*	ōh	*oh*
ȯne	*one*	ūse	*use*
ĕgg	*egg*	sĕntence	*sentence*

Lesson 16. (See Rule 4, above.)

What a dreadful storm! The wind blows a gale and the house fairly trembles. Now the clouds roll. The thunder makes the windows rattle. How dark it grows!

wĭnd	drĕadful	gāle	house	fâirly
clouds	wĭndows	răttle	rōll	grōws

Lesson 17.

Ann's dress is torn. She is a wild, careless girl. She soils her book, and does not learn her lesson well. Her doll's clothes are soiled also.

Remark.—*The apostrophe and s ('s) are often used to denote ownership or possession.*

Ann's	*Ann's*	câreless	*careless*
dŏll's	*doll's*	frock	*clothes*
drĕss	*dress*	lĕarn	*learn*
apŏstrophe	*apostrophe*	soils	*soils*
clōthes	*clothes*	tōrn	*torn*

Lesson 18. (See remark above.)

Clara's pencil is in her small wooden box. She has put her slate away. She has a place for everything. Do you think Clara is a careless girl?

Clara's	*Clara's*	wŏŏden	*wooden*
pĕncil	*pencil*	bŏŏks	*books*
smạll	*small*	plāce	*place*
awāy	*away*	gîrl	*girl*
slāte	*slate*	frāme	*frame*

Lesson 19.

The days of the week are Sunday, Monday, Tuesday, Wednesday, Thursday, Friday, and Saturday. In writing them, begin each one with a capital letter. Seven days make one week. Thirty days make one month.

Sunday Monday Tuesday Wednesday
Thursday Friday Saturday
number capital thirty

Lesson 20. — Review.

squirrel	proper	pork	number
brought	Henry	exclamation	Ann's
woods	shear	sentence	apostrophe
named	hatch	dreadful	learn
two	Bessie	window	soils
four	Queen	rattle	Wednesday
coasting	question	careless	Tuesday
question	farmer	pencil	girl
sport	James	clothes	thirty
mutton	fairly	wooden	seven

Lesson 21.

Here is a young soldier. He carries a wooden musket, a tin sword, a toy pistol, a small knap-sack and a canteen.

knăpsack	sōldier	cărries	swōrd	petwēēn
pĭstol	căntēēn	hȳphen	cŏmpound	pärts

Rule 5. — *Use a hyphen (-) between the parts of a compound word.*

Lesson 22.

(See rule above.)

grăndfather	——	snōw	*snow*
grăndmother	——.	vĭsit	*visit*
fēēble	*feeble*	lóve	*love*
lŏcks	*locks*	vĕry	*very*
whīte	*white*	wāit	*wait*

To the Teacher. — Require the pupils to use these words in original sentences.

Lesson 23.

(See Rules 3 and 5.)

See, Florence, how the snow comes down. The trees are bending with their burden of white. I like to be out in a snow-storm. Of what is the soft, white snow made? When the storm is over, we can take a sleigh-ride.

Florence down bending burden soft snow=storm sleigh=ride trees made worth

Lesson 24.

dĭnner-bell	——	cōōl	*cool*
härvest-field	——	quīte	*quite*
ạlmost	*almost*	rĭng	*ring*
been	*been*	hôrn	*horn*
Joe	*Joe*	rĕady	*ready*

Lesson 25.

Benjamin Franklin said :

"Early to bed and early to rise
Makes a man healthy, wealthy, and wise."

Rule 6. — *Enclose the words of another in quotation marks* (" ").

*early makes rise Benjamin
another healthy wealthy wise
quotation enclose*

Lesson 26.

(Review rule above.)

*Lawrence found a piece of money
in front of a man's store. He
knew it was not his own, and
having been taught to do what
was right, he called to the man
and said, "Sir, have you lost
any money ?"*

To the Teacher. — Require the pupil to select and spell the *new* words in this lesson

Lesson 27.

Grace	*Grace*	Hattie	*Hattie*
road-side	*road-side*	wạlking	*walking*
lēaves	*leaves*	läughed	*laughed*
hōme	*home*	rŭstle	*rustle*
sĕven	*seven*	twĭgs	*twigs*

To the Teacher.—Require the pupil to use these words in sentences illustrating Rule 6, page 23.

Lesson 28.

A man came by the school-house, driving a team of snow-white horses. He called out to the children, "Do you want a sleigh-ride?" We said "Yes," and got into the sleigh, huddled close together and were driven twice around the square. A merry set were we!

snōw-white	togĕther	twīce	schōol	sleigh
hŭddled	squâre	affĭrmative	mĕrry	drīving

Lesson 29.

A bright fire was blazing on the hearth. Harry was reading from a new book which his papa and mamma had given him for a birthday present. Harry was only seven, but he could read quite well, and was happy with his new book.

birthday hearth reading blazing poem Harry which knowledge present history

Lesson 30. — Review.

1. soldier	visit	ring	Grace
2. pistol	very	quite	laughed
3. carries	Florence	quotation	walking
4. sword	bending	rise	leaves
5. canteen	burden	early	huddled
6. hyphen	snow-storm	Lawrence	affirmative
7. compound	sleigh-ride	knew	merry
8. grandfather	made	piece	knowledge
9. grandmother	dinner-bell	Benjamin	road-side
10. feeble	harvest-field	money	blazing

To the Teacher.—Require the pupil to write the Review and mark the vowels from memory.

Lesson 31.

bīnd	*bind*	supper	*supper*
gärden	*garden*	mĭlk	*milk*
cloudy	*cloudy*	brĕad	*bread*
brīght	*bright*	crŭst	*crust*
plĕasant	*pleasant*	small	*milkpan*

It is pleasant to watch the farmer —— wheat into bundles. We grow potatoes in our ——. This is a —— day. I love a —— day. I sometimes eat —— and —— for supper. I have a small tin cup of my own.

Lesson 32.

sĭlver	*silver*	cŏpper	*copper*
tĭn	*tin*	zĭnc	*zinc*
īron	*iron*	plătinum	*platinum*
gōld	*gold*	potăssium	*potassium*
lĕad	*lead*	mĕrcury	*mercury*

Which is the most useful metal? Which is the most precious metal? Tell me all you can about one of these metals.

Lesson 33.

desk table clock bell eraser crayon.
pointers picture bench crayon trough

Sit erect at your ——. Our teacher keeps a neat ——.
If you listen, you will hear the —— strike. We use the
—— when we go to the black-board. A nice —— here
and there adds much to the appearance of a school-room.

Lesson 34.

I love the —— days of ——. It is then that the
sound of —— nuts is heard. The leaves change ——;
some turn red, some golden, while others grow brown
and sear.

ạutumn	*autumn*	cȯlor	*color*
mĕlancholy	*melancholy*	fôrest	*forest*
drŏpping	*dropping*	gōlden	*golden*
sound	*sound*	sēar	*sear*
tûrn	*turn*	chānge	*change*

Lesson 35.

One day Jennie's papa came home and ———— her a nice present. It was an ———— of furniture for her doll house. "How delightful!" exclaimed Jennie. What do you suppose it was that she received? It was a little ————.

brought	ärticle	delīghtful	fûrniture	cărriage
sŭpper	doll-house	Jennie's	plēased	bĕd-spread

Lesson 36.

Jennie was an industrious girl, and so she made a ——
for her ——. She —— her doll house every day. When
she ——, she folds her table-spread and puts it in her
little bureau drawer. She has a ——, a ——, a set of
small ——, and many other things in her doll-house.

table-spread sweeps week folds china stand bureau cradle broom mattress

Lesson 37.

"Mamma, where is the sun to-day
While all the rain comes down?"
"Ah! little girl
With flaxen curl,
Who has not asked before
This question o'er and o'er?

"My Dear," the mother answered back,
Her child with faith to fill,
"Behind the cloud so thick and black
The sun is shining still."

flăxen curl shīning ănswered băckward

Lesson 38.

bŭtter	chēēse	hóney	sält
bĭscuit	soup	pĕpper	sugar
crăcker	cŏffee	pĭckle	syrup

Lesson 39.

Silas is a —— boy in school. He will mark on his desk with his ——, tear his book and throw the paper upon the floor, whisper and misbehave when his teacher's back is turned. He is —— in trouble with his ——, and does not treat them kindly. So they do not love him very dearly, and he is not happy.

Silas troublesome lead-pencil frequently tears school-mates. kindly dearly misbehave hence

Lesson 40. — Review.

article	crayon	sear	wire
delightful	table	erect	crust
furniture	frequently	change	milk
faith	dearly	misbehave	cloudy
behind	appearance	lead-pencil	bright
while	schoolroom	supper	garden
pepper	autumn	boilers	copper
coffee	sound	platinum	zinc
picture	forest	horse-shoe	iron
bench	sugar	bullets	watches

Lesson 41.

drōne	*drone*	dĭsturbed	*disturbed*
wŏrking	*working*	swạrm	*swarm*
quēēn	*queen*	dọing	*doing*
câre	*care*	bēē-hive	*bee-hive*
hīve	*hive*	sĕttle	*settle*

To the Teacher.—Require the pupil to use these words in original sentences.

Lesson 42.

chĕst	lŭngs	heärt	spīne	bŏdy
stŏmach	hĕad	brāin	rĭbs	blood

The divisions of the body are the head, the trunk and the limbs. The head contains the brain. The chest contains the heart and lungs which are protected by the ribs.

Lesson 43.

The veins and the arteries carry the blood. There is little or no blood in the hair or in the nails. Breathing fresh air purifies the blood. Strong drink will make the blood impure.

ärteries	vẹins	lĭver	mŭscles	bōnes
nĕrves	skin	nāils	hâir	joints

Lesson 44.

seeing hearing feeling tasting smelling senses mind controls organs perform.

There are five senses, namely: —

sight, taste, smell, hearing, and feeling.

The eye is the organ of sight, and the ear the organ of hearing. We should take good care of the body.

Lesson 45.

schoolboy	——	jănitor	*janitor*
pūpil	*pupil*	prīmary	*primary*
stūdent	*student*	grămmar	*grammar*
lĕsson	*lesson*	depärtment	*department*
ăpplicātion	——	ĭndustry	*industry*

A —— is generally happy. A diligent —— will soon learn a hard ——. It is an honor to be perfect in —— each day. The —— will keep the room warm by keeping a good fire. A —— school is one composed of small pupils.

Lesson 46.

tärdy	prŏmpt	mĕrit	rewạrd	dĭshonor
mĕdal	pŭnctual	dĭligent	hŏnor	prōmote

The best students are seldom ——. Be —— in all you do, and —— will follow Always be —— in study, and you will succeed

Lesson 47.

căttle	hôrses	hŏgs	mūles	cälves
gōats	chĭckens	gēēse	· dŭcks	tûrkeys

I like to see a nice farm. The farmer takes delight in raising stock. ———— are very useful to the farmer. The flesh of ———— is used for food. ———— furnish feathers for pillows and beds.

Lesson 48.

pēaches	plŭms	grāpes	orchards	mĕadows
fiēlds	côrn	clŏver	stock	guĭnea

The farmer's orchard abounds in ————, ————, and ————, while his meadows and fields are rich with ————. Grapes grow on ————. Plums grow on ————. Most ———— has three leaves.

Lesson 49.

cärpenter   hăndsaw   chĭsel   plāne   măllet
tōōls   shāvings   blŏcks   rĭbbons   mōuldings

A —— has many tools. He makes long —— with a ——. They look like ——. · I love to play among the shavings, and pick up the little —— of wood that are sawed off with the ——. A —— is a hammer made of wood.

Lesson 50.—Review.

1. disturbed	honor	chisel	drawing
2. doing	department	plane	ink'stand
3. care	poultry	blocks	stock
4. heart	insect	tools	guinea
5. stomach	meadow	field	duckling
6. ribs	orchard	clover	gosling
7. tardy	ribbons	plums	veins
8. prompt	school-boy	peaches	liver
9. diligent	lesson	promote	controls
10. punctual	corn	failure	tasting

Lesson 51.

I'm	is for	I am.	don't	is for	do not.
I'll	" "	I will.	can't	" "	cannot.
I've	" "	I have.	you're	" "	you have.
he's	" "	he is.	you'll	" "	you will.
she's	" "	she is.	they'll	" "	they will.

Rule 7. — *The apostrophe (') denotes an omission, or that there has been a contraction.*

—— afraid —— be late unless I make haste.
—— a very pretty knife. My father gave it to me.
—— soon be as large as I am.
—— you love the sunshine!

Note.—Do not make frequent use of contractions.

Lesson 52.

entīre	*entire*	
rōaming	*roaming*	
vălley	*valley*	
glĕn	*glen*	
glāde	*glade*	
fōaming	*foaming*	
cătaract	*cataract*	
pōuring	*pouring*	
rōaring	*roaring*	
sĭnging	*singing*	

To the Teacher.—Require the pupils to use these words in original sentences.

Lesson 53.

An old door —— on its hinges.

The —— is overhead.

Flowers have a —— smell.

When several speak at once there is confusion.

We sometimes —— the graves of the dead by strewing flowers upon them.

Do not speak angrily or be a ——.

cŏnfūsion	scōld	frāgrant	dĕcorate	hĭckory
hĭnges	crēaks	rŭst	cēiling	māple

Lesson 54.

channel burst streamlet winding
morsel ragged scarlet blazing
striped value

The course of the —— is a —— one.

The dove makes a dainty —— for the hawk.

I love a bright, —— fire.

We often fail to appreciate the —— of time.

—— is not a desirable color for a garment.

Lesson 55.

To the Teacher.—Have the class commit the following. Teach a lesson.

Turn, turn my wheel! All life is brief,
What now is bud will soon be leaf,
What now is leaf will soon decay:
The wind blows east, the wind blows west,
The blue eggs in the robin's nest
Will soon have wings and beak, and breast,
And flutter and fly away.

—From " Song of the Potter," HENRY W. LONGFELLOW.

Lesson 56.

hanging	between	lĕvel	cliff	frŏnt
cȯvers	tŏsses	cûrly	tēēth	strāight

The cloud seemed to be ___ ___
the earth and the sky. There is
a ___ spot at the top of yonder
___ where an eagle yearly builds
her nest.

Lesson 57.

DIRECTION. — Distinguish between :

līghtning and līghtening	ăx and ăcts
gĕsture and jĕster	colonel and kernel
fĭsher and fĭssure	pour and pore
ĕmigrate and ĭmmigrate	ăffect and effect
except and accept	aloŭd and allowed

Note. — The teacher should direct attention to both the spelling and pronunciation of such words as those above, explaining the meaning and requiring sentences formed to illustrate their use.

celebration pleasant Emma aunt Helen Gertrude mamma loving holiday cannon

Lesson 58.

dēfĕnd	*defend*	dĭzzy	*dizzy*
forsāke	*forsake*	mŭddy	*muddy*
pârents	*parents*	ōcean	*ocean*
dūty	*duty*	pĕbbles	*pebbles*
protĕst	*protest*	stōre	*store*

Lesson 59.

Did you ever ——— to the top of a tall ———? I often ——— how the men build them so high. Some steeples have a vane on top of them, to show which way the wind ———.

ăscĕnd	stēēples	wŏnder	bŭĭld	blōws
wĭthin	vāne	sĕxton	wạrning	ĭnjured

Lesson 60. — Review.

disturbed	hickory	mamma	within
scarcely	roaring	parade	wonder
church	fragrant	parents	celebration
gray	ceiling	ascend	niece
arteries	cousin	pebbles	occasion
being	yesterday	murmur	gladness
sorrow	straight	defend	fathom
pleasant	prepare	begins	between
aunt	hurried	build	curly
muddy	distance	anvil	front

Lesson 61.

A miser had a lump of gold which he buried in the ground, coming to look at the spot every day. One day he found that it was stolen, and he began to tear his hair and lament loudly. A neighbor seeing him said: "Pray do not grieve so; bury a stone in the hole and fancy it is the gold. It will serve you just as well, for when the gold was there you made no use of it." —ÆSOP, "The Miser" (A Fable).

To the Teacher.—Select the *new* and difficult words, and require the pupil to spell and define.

Lesson 62.

ōwns	plows	fŏŏd	bŭggy	scāles
nēat	cŏttage	wăgon	härness	pōultry

Lesson 63.

DIRECTION. — Copy the following:

I asked the sage when wandering afar,
In search of wisdom's bright and shining star,
"What's wisdom?" He exclaimed with tearful eyes,
"The fear and love of God's the wisdom of the wise."

See Rule 7, p. 36.

wĭsdom shīning sāge wandering tạlking

Lesson 64.

"But where shall wisdom be found?
And where is the place of understanding?
Man knoweth not the price thereof,
Neither is it found in the land of the living;
The deep saith It is not in me,
And the sea saith It is not in me;
It can not be gotten for gold,
Neither can silver be weighed for the price thereof."

To the Teacher. — Select the *new* and difficult words, and require the pupil to spell and define.

Lesson 65.

DIRECTION. — Copy the following:

Flag of the free hearts' only home,
By angel hands to valor given;
Thy stars have lit the welkin dome,
And all thy hues were born in heaven.
Forever float that standard sheet!
Where breathes the foe but falls before us,
With freedom's soil beneath our feet,
And freedom's banner streaming o'er us?

—J. R. DRAKE.

Lesson 66.

flăttery	bŭtcher	ŭpright	consŭlts
compâre	cŭnning	hŏnorable	stŭtter
ănecdotes	ĭmitates	truthful	fälter
mŏnkey	hȳpocrite	indŭstrious	hĕsitate
acôrn	prĕcipice	căptive	dŭsty

Many —— are told about the monkey. He is said to be a very —— animal, and to —— the actions of persons. He is a very nimble animal, and lives in the forest. He eats nuts and fruits, and sometimes flesh.

Lesson 67.

scrāper	slēēp	a̤uger	grānary
thrĕad	fĕnces	sĭster	mānger
thĭmble	scȳthe	shăggy	trôugh
nēēdle	hărrow	ēating	stȳ
o'clock	bēing	sew (so)	fowls

A farmer will make a pond with a scraper or bore a hole with an ——. I can use ——, ——, and ——, and sew almost as well as ——. Carlo has long, shaggy hair. He is a watch-dog.

Lesson 68.

kĭndness	requīred	descrībe	lōad	sŏngster
assĭst	mȏrning	ēvening	mĭdnight	grief

Hark! the lark will —— a sweet song.
Who can —— the beauties of a —— scene?
A young horse will draw a heavy ——
At noon the sun is overhead.
When the heart is full of sympathy and love, the hands can always find something to do. Can you define the word "nimble"?

Lesson 69.

Jan.	is for	January.	July	is for	July.
Feb.	" "	February.	Aug.	" "	August.
Mar.	" "	March.	Sept.	" "	September.
Apr.	" "	April.	Oct.	" "	October.
May	" "	May.	Nov.	" "	November.
June	" "	June.	Dec.	" "	December.

Thirty days hath September, April, June, and November,
All the rest have thirty-one, save February, which alone
Hath twenty-eight, and one day more
We add to it one year in four.

Lesson 70.

anxious	search	trough	shoes
destroy	plastering	hosiery	shawls
nephew	finished	cunning	honorable
property	gingham	industrious	stutter
sleek	compare	falter	hesitate
buggy	monkey	listen	billows
shining	hypocrite	midnight	evening
living	prints	auger	scythe
incendiary	nimble	shaggy	thimble
manger	skittish	February	December

Lesson 71.

Kansas City, Mo.,
July 10, 1891.

Messrs. D. C. Heath & Co.,
Boston, Mass.

Gentlemen:—

The books you shipped us were duly received. They were in good condition and we were highly pleased with them. Find enclosed a check for the money, forty-five dollars ($45.00) in payment.

Yours truly,

H. O. Palen.

shĭpped	condĭtion	enclōsed	recēived	dŏllars
fāilure	forty-five	chärts	glōbes	pāyment

Lesson 72.

The ____ tree has a showy, snow-white blossom. A conifer is a tree or plant that bears cones. Did you ever see a ____ growing on a pine tree? On what part of the stalk is the blossom of the corn found? Do elm trees bear seeds? Do pine trees?

cătălpä	prĭmrose	dăndelion	dāisy	sēarch
cōnifer	flower	blŏssom	shōwy	wander.ng

Lesson 73.

Plants furnish shelter, raiment, food, and medicine. We make furniture and machinery of wood, and paper of bark and other substances. Bark was at one time used by the Indians of North America for making small boats or canoes. Plants assist in purifying the air, and are the chief source of fuel.

fûrnish	Indians	pūrifying	shāde
rāiment	māking	fūel	ornaments
mĕdicine	sōurce	pāper	cōal
māchĭnery	canŏes	plănts	wŏŏd
America	assĭst	fûrniture	shĕlter

Lesson 74.

U.S.	is for	United States.	Benj.	is for	Benjamin.
Mo.	" "	Missouri.	Chas.	" "	Charles.
Ill.	" "	Illinois.	Jas.	" "	James.
Io.	" "	Iowa.	Thos.	" "	Thomas.
Ind.	" "	Indiana.	Geo.	" "	George.
Kan.	" "	Kansas.	Wm.	" "	William.
N.Y.	" "	New York.	Sam'l	" "	Samuel.
Co.	" "	Company.	Jno.	" "	John.
Co.	" "	County.	Alex.	" "	Alexander.
Pa.	" "	Pennsylvania.	Chris.	" "	Christopher.

Lesson 75.

wĭthout	bĕrries	shĭngles	rădishes
spīces	bēams	pōsts	lĕttuce
bŭlbs	lŭmber	ònions	spĭnach
chiēfly	brĭdges	potātoes	cĕl'ery
bärns	pŭmps	châirs	mĕdicine

Lesson 76.

sträw	flăx	dūrable	jūte	gŏs'samer
cŏtton	hĕmp	fāmous	prŏducts	rŭbber

Lesson 77.

wȯnderful	hăppily	crēatures	nĕcessary	togĕther
fămilies	piēces	wĭlling	decīde	sĕparate

Beavers are good carpenters, dam-builders, and plasterers. These lively little animals can do a —— amount of hard work. They live very —— together. If they —— to build a dam, they cut or gnaw down shrubs or small trees on the bank of the stream, and use them in making the dam.

Lesson 78.

mănner	*manner*	
câreful	*careful*	
brănches	*branches*	
flōat	*float*	
ănimals	*animals*	

mŭsk'-răt	*musk-rat*
ŏtter	*otter*
mĭnk	*mink*
răccoon	*raccoon*
opŏs'sum	*opossum*

The musk-rat, like the beaver, is fond of the water. Musk-rats build their houses in the same manner that beavers do. · Both animals furnish fur for man's use. Fur animals usually live in a cold climate.

Lesson 79.

It is extremely cold in the —— regions. The ——
is found there. Hear the —— shout of the huntsman
when he brings down his game! The people who live
in the far north wear fur clothing through the long,
dreary winters. In such dress they look uncouth, but
many of them are good people.

ärctic	*arctic*	wändering	*wandering*
rẹindeer	*reindeer*	uncọuth	*uncouth*
joyous	*joyous*	lēisure	*leisure*
afär	*afar*	advăntage	*advantage*
dĭstance	*distance*	lĭving	*living*

Lesson 80. — Review.

received	lettuce	bridges	U.S. = ?
duly	leisure	chiefly	Ill. = ?
wonderful	piece	without	Benj. = ?
necessary	creatures	shipped	Kan. = ?
taking	decide	enclosed	Sam'l = ?
arctic	showy	avenue	Jno. = ?
conifer	catalpa	celery	Thos. = ?
shingles	medicine	gossamer	Jas. = ?
radishes	machinery	careful	Mo. = ?
spinach	purifying	happily	Co. = ?

Lesson 81.

A.M.	is for	Master of Arts.	a.m.	is for	before noon.
P.M.	" "	Post Master.	p.m.	" "	after noon.
C.O.D.	" "	cash on delivery.	Prof.	" "	Professor.
cts.	" "	cents.	ft.	" "	feet.

Note to the Teacher.—Require the pupils to use these abbreviations in original sentences.

Lesson 82.

consĕnt	*consent*	gĕnuine	*genuine*
attāin	*attain*	pŭlley	*pulley*
mĭngle	*mingle*	news-boy	*news-boy*
estātes	*estates*	lạunder	*launder*
permĭssion	*permission*	gĕntry	*gentry*

The pupil asks ____ and the teacher gives ____ . Do not ____ with bad people. The ____ of Europe are wealthy people. They live on large ____ . We should strive to ____ a high degree of excellence.

Lesson 83.

Ark. is for *Arkansas,* (ARKANSAW)   *R.R.* is for *Rail Road*
Neb. "   *Nebraska*   *p.* "   *page*
Cal. "   *California*   *p.p.* "   *pages*
Colo. "   *Colorado*   *doz* "   *dozen*
N.M. "   *New Mexico*   *pk.* "   *peck*

tyro	ălto	stăff	mĕlody	begĭnner
tĕnor	soprä́no	nōtes	musĭcian	cord

Lesson 84.

DIRECTION. — Copy the script.

blĕnded	rĕsts	bāss	clĕff	härmony
mūsic	hōlds	dĭscord	slurs	bärs

You must wake and call me early,
Call me early, mother dear;
For to-morrow'll be the happiest time
Of all the glad New Year:
Of all the glad New Year, mother,
The maddest, merriest day,
For I'm to be Queen o' the May, mother,
I'm to be Queen o' the May.

—TENNYSON, " The May Queen."

Lesson 85.

dĭngy	*dingy*	sŭnshine	*sunshine*
cŏbwebs	*cobwebs*	sŭnbeam	*sunbeam*
bĭns	*bins*	sŭnset	*sunset*
thrĭfty	*thrifty*	sŭnstroke	*sunstroke*
ĭndolent	*indolent*	sŭnrise	*sunrise*

Lesson 86.

scoop-shovel	spŏnge	piäno	pineapple
bälmy	gōpher	flūte	sour
ăcid	grīndstone	jewsharp	bĭtter
ăcrid	gōphermound	guĭtar'	jūice

A____ wind blows from the southern sea. A____ digs in the ground. A lemon has an ____ or ____ taste. The ____ grows in the sea. The ____ is a fruit that somewhat resembles a pine cone in shape.

Lesson 87.

DIRECTION. — Copy the script:

"Turn, turn, my wheel! turn round and round,
Without a pause, without a sound:
So spins the flying world away!
This clay, well mixed with marl and sand,
Follows the motion of my hand;
For some must follow, some command,
Though all are made of clay!"

—LONGFELLOW, "Song of the Potter."

| pause | spĭns | sănd | märl | mĭneral |
| cŏmmand | clāy | mĭxed | fŏllows | mōtion |

Lesson 88.

A ____ spins a web at the ____ of
its den. Insects that ____ to come
too near are ____ in this web, and
thus become easy prey for the
spider.

chănce   spīder   ĕntrance   entăn'gle   vĕnture

Lesson 89.

stÿle	*style*	păr'asŏl	*parasol*
ĕlegant	*elegant*	courtesy	*courtesy*
expensive	*expensive*	gĕnerous	*generous*
furnished	*furnished*	clōthing	*clothing*
lĭving	*living*	bŭttons	*buttons*

Lesson 90. — Review.

thrifty	attain	entrance	A.M.	= ?
balmy	genuine	entangle	P.M.	= ?
sunset	estate	millet	A.M.	= ?
harvest	news-boy	saying	P.M.	= ?
gopher	bars	venture	C.O.D.	= ?
piano	launder	parasol	ft.	= ?
melody	generous	sponge	doz.	= ?
consent	fully	acid	R.R.	= ?
harmony	jewsharp	acrid	p.	= ?
courtesy	grindstone	bins	pp.	= ?
insects	marl	command	pk.	= ?
follows	mineral	pineapple	Prof.	= ?

Lesson 91.

moŏnlight	dĭstance	spāce	mēans
stärs	ăppear	trăvels	fĭxed
twĭnkle	togĕther	păsses	reflĕcted
mĭdday	apärt	gŏverns	account
shīne	glădness	understanding	o'clock

I love a —— night. I like to watch the stars as they appear, one by one, in the sky. They are at a great distance from us, and —— small on that account, but they are very large. Our earth travels through ——. God governs all.

Lesson 92.

skylärk	*skylark*	wĭgwam	*wigwam*
chĭmney	*chimney*	rĕgular	*regular*
swạllows	*swallows*	retīre	*retire*
pŏnder	*ponder*	dĭssolve	*dissolve*
tēarful	*tearful*	bĭllows	*billows*

Lesson 93.

*precious acknowledge judgment infringe
mindful stubborn earnestly revived
copious perverse faithful merchant.
bewildered hasty succeed afford*

Truth is more precious than gold; hence be —— and speak the truth. A —— rain fell and revived vegetation. The traveller —— that he was entirely —— and could not find his way. Do not be —— or ——. Strive earnestly, use good ——, and you are likely to ——. Do not —— on the rights of others. A —— cannot —— to sell goods at cost.

Lesson 94.

*gardener thoughtless persuade lamplight
gaslight complain corrode apricot
overcome banish cheerful.*

A —— once let a —— boy into his garden. The boy meant well enough, but was so thoughtless as to pluck some buds from some choice plants. Do not persuade anyone to engage in wrong-doing. Iron will —— if exposed to the weather.

Lesson 95.

parĕn'tal	*parental*	prĕmises	*premises*
encrōach	*encroach*	dĭscover	*discover*
affĕction	*affection*	pärtisan	*partisan*
patience	*patience*	enrăpture	*enrapture*
hụrräh	*hurrah*	aflōat	*afloat*

Lesson 96.

life-boat   dăshes   chēēred   sĭngle-handed   därkly

They're is for *they are; we'll* is for *we will; 'twas* is for *it was.*

"Hurrah! the life-boat dashes on,
Though darkly the reef may frown;
The rock is there, the ship is gone
Full twenty fathoms down.
But, cheered by hope the seamen cope
With the billows, single-handed;
They're all in the boat. Hurrah! they're afloat!
And now they are safely landed
By the life-boat! Cheer the life-boat!"

Lesson 97.

cŏŏper	hămmer	jeweler	pĭncers
pāinter	brŭsh	shoemaker	knīfe
prĭnter	tȳpe	bärber	rāzor
mĭlliner	nēēdle	tāilor	scĭssors

Lesson 98.

cŏvey	globular	flĭnty	surmount
pärtridge	pĕnetrate	prōpound'	contract
sĕntinel	prĕssure	dĭfficult	mĭller
mănner	survey'	bärley	flĭmsy

A ___ of birds flew over. A ___ is
a plump bird. The ___ remained
upon the watch until morning.
The ___ of water may be so great
as to burst an iron pipe.
A hunter will ___ a dense forest
in search of game. Learn to ___
all difficulties.

Lesson 99.

hẽrmit	alōne	ĭntercourse	secluded.
devotes	interrupted	meditation	religious

*A ___ is one who lives in some ___
spot and sometimes even in a cave.
In this condition he has but little
___ with his fellowmen. Often the
hermit ___ himself to some ___
question. He probably lives alone
that he may not be ___ in his*

Lesson 100. — Review.

governs	knife	earnestly	hurrah
regular	difficult	precious	clashes
reflected	flimsy	hasty	patience
faithful	sinful	bewilder	encroach
carnestly	beware	copious	secluded
partisan	merchant	apricot	pressure
premises	infringe	corrode	mariner
single-handed	judgment	lamplight	milliner
scissors	succeed	persuade	penetrate
razor	perverse	cheerful	barley

PART II.

THE PROGRESSIVE SPELLER.

Lesson 101.

âir, *the atmosphere.*	āte, *did eat.*
heir, *one who inherits.*	eight, *twice four.*
ạll, *the whole.*	bĕll, *a sounding vessel.*
awl, *a tool.*	belle, *a beautiful young lady.*
ärk, *a vessel.*	be, *to exist.*
arc, *part of a circumference.*	bee, *an insect.*

Lesson 102.

frīghten	brĭttle	blŭster	rōgue
mīldew	quĭlt	crĭmson	hạlter
rīvalry	blănket	salūte	lăntern
jāiler	cŭrtain	commảnder	schĕdule
quĭcken	pạuse	stūpid	allow

To the Teacher. — Require original sentences to be formed, illustrating the meaning and use of the words in this lesson.

63

Lesson 103.

cōld	frĭgid	wĭther	făstened
bûrn	blŭbber	sāfely	secūrely
scôrch	bŭbble	conclūded	fĭnished
wĭlt	condĭtion	rĕfuge	lōōsened

The traveler took —— behind the rock. After due consideration, I —— to make the effort. It is very —— in the frigid zone, and sailors, while there, frequently use the fat of the whale, called ——, for food. The thrifty farmer will keep his stock in good ——.

Lesson 104.

sīlent	*silent*	lĭberty	*liberty*
whĭrl-wind	*whirl-wind*	ôrator	*orator*
consĭgned	*consigned*	sădness	*sadness*
phōtograph	*photograph*	berēavement	*bereavement*
sĭngular	*singular*	anxiety	*anxiety*

It is sometimes best to be ——. I once saw a —— sight; it was a —— passing along, and taking leaves and straw far up into the air.

A certain —— once said, "Give me liberty or give me death!"

Lesson 105.

ball, *a sphere.*
bawl, *to cry aloud.*
bāse, *vile, mean.*
bass, *a part in music.*
clīmb, *to mount.*
clime, *a region.*

cĕnt, *a coin.*
sent, *did send.*
scent, *a smell.*
beâr, *to carry.*
bear, *an animal.*
bare, *naked.*

Never do a —— deed. My friend sings ——. The child was —— to the store with a —— to buy a needle. A —— can —— a tree. The sailor goes to many a foreign ——.

Lesson 106.

lōwland	scrāper	flourish	rejĕct
stāble	lĕvee	pursūit	explōde
mĕasure	sālesman	ĕnemy	tobăcco
sīlence	bȳ-gŏne	ärmy	powder
ōverflow	retûrned	retrēat	rīfle

To the Teacher. —These words may be defined and used in sentences.

Lesson 107.

Blanche	Laura	Martin	Wilber
Ella	Olive	Cyrus	Julius
Flora	Adelia	Clarence	Robert
Julia	Gertrude	Donaldson	Benjamin
Meda	Della	Filmore	Delbert

Lesson 108.

Rule 8. — *All proper adjectives (words derived from proper names) should begin with a capital letter.*

PROPER NOUN.	PROPER ADJ.	PROPER NOUN.	PROPER ADJ.
America	American	Alps	Alpine
Ireland	Irish	Africa	African
Germany	German	Spain	Spanish
Russia	Russian	Asia	Asiatic
Greece	Grecian	Rome	Roman

Lesson 109.

rŭgged	valïse	pärcel	bŭndle
lābel	bŏttle	whĭp-cord	fought
săchel	drŭggist	cŏnstant	perpĕtual
trăveler	drŭgs	brăvely	dâring

To the Teacher. — These words may be defined and used in sentences.

Lesson 110.

M.S. is for manuscript.
N.B. " " take notice.
8vo. " " octavo.
12mo. " " duodecimo.
4to. " " quarto.

et. al. is for "and others."
B.C. " " Before Christ.
Mr. " " Mister.
Mrs. " " Mistress.
Rem. " " Remainder.

Lesson 111.

clause, *part of a sentence.*
claws, *nails of an animal.*
cŏarse, *not fine.*
course, *direction.*
cĕll, *a small room.*
sĕll, *to dispose of.*

dew, *moisture.*
due, *what is owing.*
dȯne, *finished.*
dun, *a color.*
deer, *an animal.*
dear, *costly, precious.*

Lesson 112.

frighten	securely	halter	bear	B.C.
brittle	salesman	lantern	cell	N.B.
loosened	levee	ball	air	Mrs.
orator	commander	cent	arc	8vo.
bravely	blanket	bass	eight	12mo
measure	rivalry	done	bee	4to.
by-gone	salute	deer	belle	M.S.
lowland	crimson	claws	awl	Mr.

Lesson 113.

gāit, *manner of walking.*	hail, *frozen rain; to salute.*
gate, *a kind of door.*	hale, *hearty; sound.*
flour, *ground grain.*	peal, *a loud noise.*
flower, *a blossom.*	peel, *to strip off the bark.*
heal, *to cure.*	hire, *wages.*
heel, *part of the foot.*	higher, *loftier.*

Lesson 114.

Rule 9. — *Most abbreviations should begin with a capital letter and be followed by a period.*

Fr.   is for France or French.

Lat.   " " Latin or Latitude.

N.A.   " " North America.

S.A.   " " South America.

D.C.   " " District of Columbia.

C.O.D.   " " Collect on Delivery.

Long.   " " Longitude.

St.   " " Saint or Street.

Ind.T.   " " Indian Territory.

Lesson 115.

Sun. - Sunday.   Cav. - Cavalry.
Mon. - Monday.   Capt. - Captain.
Tues. - Tuesday.   Col. - Colonel.
Wed. - Wednesday.   Hon. - Honorable.
Th. - Thursday.   Lieut. - Lieutenant.
Fri. - Friday.   Supt. - Superintendent.
Sat. - Saturday.   P.O. - Post Office.

Lesson 116.

trĭbute	skĕleton	tĕnder	bĕlfry
pĕrish	trīumph	behōld	härbor
thĭcket	achiēve	shăllow	hĕctic
succĕss	cărrying	blĕmish	beautiful
hŭnger	drīving	frĕshet	ēasily

Lesson 117.

dĭligent	stūdious	amūsing	lïughable
āble	cŏmpetent	fīrm	sŏlid
nōted	distĭnguished	sŭbstăntial	endūring
hīght	ăltitude	permĭssion	prĭvilege
griēve	bewāil	predĭct	foretĕll

Lesson 118.

exămine	obsĕrve	expōsed	Atlantic
ōpenings	păssages	dānger	Pacific
ŭnder	benēath	mŏsses	Indian
attăches	grōws	through	gŭlfs
dīve	sĕarch	ănimals	wạters

—— the sponge on your desk. —— the small ——
in it. It is an animal, and these openings are small
—— through which food may pass to all parts of the
body. The sponge —— in water. Men —— deep down
into the sea in —— of the sponge. In so doing, they
are —— to great ——. Sponges are found in the warm
waters of the ——, ——, and —— oceans.

Lesson 119.

reign, *to rule.*
rāin, *water from clouds.*
stāke, *a post; a sum raised.*
steāk, *a slice of meat.*
bēach, *the seashore.*
beech, *a kind of tree.*
beat, *to strike.*
beet, *a vegetable.*
flea, *an insect.*
flee, *to run away.*

Lesson 120.

bow, *to bend the body.*
bough, *the branch of a tree.*
bĭn, *a box.*
been, *existed.*
rye, *a kind of grain.*
wry, *twisted.*
sȯme, *a few, a part.*
sum, *the amount.*
grōan, *a moan.*
grown, *increased.*

Lesson 121.

Ala. – Alabama.	Miss. – Mississippi.
Ariz. – Arizona.	Nev. – Nevada.
Conn. – Connecticut.	N.J. – New Jersey.
Del. – Delaware.	N.H. – New Hampshire.
Fla. – Florida.	N.C. – North Carolina.
Ga. – Georgia.	Me. – Maine.
Md. – Maryland.	Mass. – Massachusetts.
Minn. – Minnesota.	N.M. – New Mexico.
Wash. – Washington.	Wyo. – Wyoming.

Lesson 122.

REVIEW OF ABBREVIATIONS.

Long.	= Longitude.	Sun.	=	?
St.	= Saint or Street.	Mon.	=	?
S.A.	= South America.	Tues.	=	?
N.A.	= North America.	Wed.	=	?
Lat.	= Latin or Latitude.	Th.	=	?
Fr.	= France or French.	Fri.	=	?
C.O.D.	= Collect on Delivery.	Sat.	=	?
D.C.	= District of Columbia.	Hon.	=	?
Ind. T.	= Indian Territory.	Supt.	=	?

Lesson 123.

Alaska = Alaska. Gen. = General.
Dak. = Dakota Gov. = Governor.
Idaho = Idaho. Esq. = Esquire.
Utah = Utah. Messrs. = Gentlemen.
Mont. = Montana. Dr. = Doctor or Debtor

Lesson 124.

Acct. = Account. Mdse. = Merchandise.
do. = ditto, or the same. No. = Number.
@. = at or per. & Co. = and Company.
% = per cent. Rec'd. = Received.
$ = Dollar or dollars. Cr. = Creditor.

Lesson 125.

Vol.	= Volume.	N.	= North.
bu.	= bushel or bushels.	bbl.	= barrel or barrels.
qt.	= quart or quarts.	hhd.	= hogshead.
oz.	= ounce or ounces.	ult.	= last, or last month.
gal.	= gallon or gallons.	inst.	= present month.

Lesson 126.

Words spelled alike, but pronounced differently and having different meanings: —

ĕs'côrt (n.), *a guard.*
escort' (v.), *to accompany.*
dĕs'ert (n.), *a barren waste.*
desẽrt' (v.), *merit; to forsake.*
cŏn'vert (n.), *one converted.*
convẽrt' (v.), *to change.*

cŏn'tract (n.), *an agreement.*
contrăct' (v.), *to draw together.*
cŏn'vict (n.), *one convicted.*
convĭct' (v.), *to prove guilty.*
fẽr'ment (n.), *a tumult.*
fermĕnt'(v.), *to set in motion.*

They sent an —— with the prisoner. The guide will —— the party to the summit of the mountain. Did you ever see a ——? Do not —— your friends. The minister led the —— to the altar. A sound argument will —— an unbeliever.

Lesson 127.

rĕb'el (n.), *one who rebels.*
rebĕl' (v.), *to rise up against.*
ŏb'ject (n.), *purpose; thing.*
objĕct' (v.), *to oppose.*
cŏn'duct (n.), *behavior.*
condŭct' (v.), *to lead.*
sŭb'ject (n.), *a topic; a follower.*

subjĕct' (v.), *to place under.*
trăns'port (n.), *joy.*
transpōrt' (v.), *to convey across.*
ĭm'port (n.), *what is brought in from abroad.*
impōrt' (v.), *to bring from abroad.*

Lesson 128.

Definition.—*Singular number denotes one person or thing. Plural number denotes more than one person or thing.*

Note.—The plural of many nouns may be formed by adding *s* to the singular.

SINGULAR.	PLURAL.	SINGULAR.	PLURAL.
stĭck	sticks	rĭver	rivers
hĕad	heads	rōad	roads
hour	hours	hŏŏp	hoops
friĕnd	friends	dŭck	ducks
păssenger	passengers	bŏnnet	bonnets

Lesson 129.

Note.—The plural of many nouns may be formed by adding *es* to the singular.

SINGULAR.	PLURAL.	SINGULAR.	PLURAL.
church	churches	màss	masses
potāto	potatoes	flăsh	flashes
tomāto	tomatoes	pēach	peaches
cōach	coaches	gràss	grasses
làss	lasses	lŏss	losses

To the Teacher.—Require the pupil to use these words in original sentences, in both the singular and the plural form.

Lesson 130.

Rule 10. — *The plural of nouns ending in y, preceded by a consonant, is usually formed by changing the y into i and adding es.*

SINGULAR.	PLURAL.	SINGULAR.	PLURAL.
căndy	candies	părty	parties
stōry	stories	pŏppy	poppies
county	counties	bĕlfry	belfries
penny	pennies	skȳ	skies
cherry	cherries	flȳ	flies

Lesson 131.

Rule 11. — *Nouns ending in y, preceded by a vowel, form the plural in the usual way, by adding s to the singular.*

SINGULAR.	PLURAL.	SINGULAR.	PLURAL.
món'key	monkeys	sûr'vey	surveys
jŏckey	jockeys	mŏney	moneys
dŏn'key	donkeys	dōorway	doorways
chimney	chimneys	frāy	frays

Cherr— turn red when they ripen. Grandpa often tells me interesting stor— about the war. —— are cunning little animals.

Lesson 132.

Rule 12. — *The plural of most nouns ending in f or fe is formed by changing f into v and adding s or es.*

SINGULAR.	PLURAL.	SINGULAR.	PLURAL.
wīfe	wives	wha̧rf	wharves
līfe	lives	shēaf	sheaves
lōaf	loaves	bēēf	beeves
wo̧lf	wolves	thiēf	thieves

Lesson 133. — Review.

To the Teacher. — Require the pupil to write plurals to the following singular nouns and give the rules.

cärpet	ŏffice	măttress	quantity
brōōm	cŏllege	looking-glass	nūrsery
bōwl	dĭpper	crŏss	hĕnnery
bărrel	cushion	bŭnch	beauty
pōker	cóverlet	wrĕnch	vănity
būreau	counter	lŭnch	sŭlky

Lesson 134.

Note. — The plurals of some nouns are not formed by any rule, but must be learned by practice.

ŏx	oxen	măn	men
gōōse	geese	mouse	mice
chīld	children	ĭndex	ĭn'dicēs
fŏŏt	feet	ăxis	ax'ēs

Lesson 135.

MALE.	FEMALE.	MALE.	FEMALE.
ăctor	ăctress	hŭsband	wīfe
author	authoress	kĭng	quēēn
Jew	Jewess	lăd	làss
gȯvernor	governess	băchelor	māid
wĭdower	wĭdow	lăndlord	lăndlady
hēro	hĕr'oine	màster	mĭstress

Note. — Fill blanks with proper words from the list above.

An —— may be an —— of his own production. The man who will face danger for the right is a ——; and the woman who does a brave act is a ——. A good —— will seek the welfare of his people.

Lesson 136.

lĭnks, *parts of a chain.*

lўnx, *an animal.*

foul, *unfair means.*

fowl, *a bird.*

knōw, *to understand.*

no, *not ; a word of denial.*

hōly, *sacred.*

wholly, *entirely.*

crēak, *to make a harsh sound.*

crēēk, *a small stream.*

wāit, *to stay.*

weight, *heaviness.*

prāy, *to entreat.*

prey, *plunder ; to plunder.*

kĭll, *to slay.*

kĭln, *an oven or pit.*

Lesson 137.

rēad, *to call words.*
rēēd, *a slender stem.*
dīe, *to expire; a stamp.*
dye, *a color.*
fōrth, *forward.*
fourth, *next after third.*
hew, *to cut.*
hue, *a color.*

earn, *to gain.*
ųrn, *a vase or vessel.*
slāy, *to kill.*
slẹigh, *a vehicle.*
pāil, *a bucket.*
pale, *white.*
hâre, *an animal.*
hâir, *of the head.*

Lesson 138.

—— on her urn, "A broken heart." Go —— and battle for the right. "—— to the line, and let the chips fall where they will." Break not a —— in memory's golden chain. An honest man will strive to —— his living.

Lesson 139.

Note.— Supply the letters omitted.

—ew —ork City is in N.Y.
—hicago is in Ill.
—hiladelphia is in Penn.
—rooklyn is on Long Island.
—uffalo is in N.Y.
—oston· is in Mass.
—incinnati is in Ohio.
—ew —r'leans is in La.

—an —rancisco is in Cal.
—aint —ouis is in Mo.
—aris is in Fr.
—ondon is in Eng.
—erlin is in Germany.
—ekin is in China.
—alcutta is in India.
—ienna is in Austria.

Lesson 140.

A REVIEW OF VOWELS WITH PRACTICE.

1. ā long (*macron*), as in hāste, slāve, mātron, āpricot.
2. ă short (*breve*), as in pătter, knăck, mătch, twăng.
3. ä Italian (*dieresis*), as in ärm, färm, äunt, cälm, läugh.
4. ạ broad (..), as in broạd, fạlse, wạlk, gạuze, fạwn, cạught.
5. à intermediate (*period*), as in fàst, bàsket, dànce, cràft, chànce.
6. â long before r (*caret*), as in câre, châir, weâr, âir, sweâr, lâir.
7. ạ like short ŏ (*period*), as in whạt, quạrrel, quạff, wạnder, wạtch.

Lesson 141.

1. ē long, as in wē, wēasel, squēak, snēēze, kēy, pēople.
2. ĕ short, as in mĕt, guĕss, dĕath, swĕat, frĕt, ĕthics.
3. ê long before r, as in whêre, hêir, wêar, pêar, thêre.
4. ẽ intermediate, as in hẽr, hẽrb, ẽrmine, hẽard, fẽrn.
5. e̱ like long a, as in the̱y, fe̱ign, pre̱y, e̱ight, conve̱y.

Lesson 142.

1. ī long, as in īce, īvory, spīne, hīreling, drīve, wīden.
2. ĭ short, as in hĭckory, thĭck, whĭp, wrĭtten, wĭcket, lĭp.
3. ï like long e, as in polïce, machïne, pïque, marïne.
4. î like ẽ, as in sîr, bîrd, vîrtue.

Lesson 143.

1. ō long, as in nōte, stōre, fōrum, cōmb, flōat, hōme.
2. ŏ short, as in ŏdd, spŏt, tŏrrid, resŏlved, bŏther, nŏt.
3. ȯ like short u, as in ȯther, dȯne, brȯther, cȯvert.
4. ọ like long oo, as in prọve, tọmb, mọve, adọ, tọurist.
5. ǫ like short oo, as in wǫlf, wǫman.
6. ô like broad a, as in ôrder, fôrm, ôrnament, accôrd.
7. ōō long, as in mōōn, bōōth, spōōn, rōōf, fōōd.
8. ŏŏ short, as in wŏŏl, fŏŏt, cŏŏp, sŏŏt, stŏŏd.

Lesson 144.

1. ū long, as in ūnite, addūce, mūte, pūny, tūne.
2. ŭ short, as in hŭbbub, scrŭb, rŭbber, flŭtter.
3. ụ like short oo, as in cụshion, bụllet, pụlpit.
4. ụ after r, as in rụde, frụit, pursụe, scrụple.
5. û before r, as in bûrn, cûrfew, tûrn, distûrb.

Lesson 145.

1. ȳ long like ī, as in flȳ, stȳle, hȳphen, tȳpe.
2. ў short like ĭ, as in lўmph, gўpsy, phўsic, abўss.

Note 1. — w is unmarked. Diphthongs (two vowels united into one sound) are unmarked. oi and oy are diphthongs, as in oil, boy; ou and ow are diphthongs, as in out, now.

Note 2. — All the letters except the vowels are called consonants. Consonants are letters that represent sounds made by the obstructed voice and by the breath.

Note 3. — The vowels are sometimes called vocals. The consonants that are sounded by the obstructed breath are called sub-vocals.

Note 4. — The consonants that represent breath sounds are called aspirates.

Lesson 146.

TABLE OF CONSONANTS.

Sub-vocals.	*Aspirates.*
b	p
ç soft (= s), cedilla ç, as in çent.	t
	k
e hard (= k), as in eall.	h
d	ch (unmarked), as in child.
ḡ hard.	çh soft(= sh), as in çhaise.
ġ soft (j in jem).	eh hard (= k), as in ehorus.
l	fh sharp, as in fhin.
m	f
n	s sharp, as in same.
r	sh
ş soft (= z), in haş.	
fh soft, or vocal, as in fhis.	
v	
w	
x (= ks or gz).	
y when a consonant.	
z in zone.	
z in azure.	

To the Teacher. — In practicing these sounds, the position of the vocal organs should be explained. Lists of words may be selected, and the consonants as well as the vowels may be marked whenever marking is necessary to distinguish the sound required for correct pronunciation.

Lesson 147.

ç soft (*cedilla*) in çensus	= s sharp in sĕldom.
ç " " çigar	= s " " sĭgnal.
ç " " deçimal	= s " " dĕstined.
ç " " çentral	= s " " sĕntiment.
ç " " çylinder	= s " " sўlvan.
ç " " çistern	= s " " sāfety.
ç " " çent	= s " " sĕlfish.
ç " " çelery	= s " " selĕct.
ç " " elïçit	= s " " rĕgister.
ç " " reçiting	= s " " sĭtting.

Lesson 148.

c hard and ch like k.		ch soft like sh.	
			(Pronounced)
colony	chorus	çhĭvalry	(shĭvalry)
crowded	chronic	çhaise	(shāze)
calvary	choleric	çhămois	(shămmy)
culprit	christen	çhăndelier	(shăndeleer')
côral	chrōnŏlogy	charāde'	(sharāde)
cūrfew	Christmas	chïcāne'	(shĕ-kāne)

To the Teacher. — Require the proper letters supplied in the following words, with diacritical marks.

—offee, —loth, —horus, —ost, offi—e, lu—id, s—orn, —alm, mustä—e, —opy, —ravat.

Lesson 149.

ş soft (ᷟ *suspended macron*) in	nipperş	= z in lizard.
ş "	" asheş	= z " blĭzzard.
ş "	" bambooş	= z " ooze.
ş "	" propōşe'	= z " zōne.
ş "	" extremeş	= z " dózen.
ş "	" amuşement	= z " frenzy.
ş "	" historieş	= z " realize.
ş "	" echoeş	= z " prĭze.
ş "	" enemieş	= z " grĭzzly.
ş "	" zeroş	= z " zeros.

Lesson 150.

ḡ hard.	ġ soft (= j).	dġ (= j).	
ḡûrgle	lŏdġement	brĭdġe	cājōle
ḡŏssip	lēġion	drŭdġe	jū'bilee
ḡĭrlish	ġĕnder	bădġer	jăcket
ḡăses	ġrănt	grŭdġe	jūice
ḡrōcery	ăġile	trŭdġe	conjĕct'ure
nēḡro	evănġelişt	wĕdġe	conjoin

To the Teacher.—Require the pupil to supply the proper letter in the following words, with diacritical marks.

bu—le, —ander, lar—est, banda—e, indi—ent, li—a-ment, fra—ment, a—itate, —ocund, —oist, —ailer, fled—e, sled—e.

Lesson 151.

DEFINITION 1. — A primitive word is one not derived from another word in the same language; as man, safe, tell.

2. — A prefix is a letter, syllable or word placed at the beginning of a primitive or root word; as ar, un, fore.

3. — A suffix is a letter, syllable or word placed at the ending of a word; as ly, er, less.

4. — A derivative word is one formed from a primitive word by means of a prefix or suffix, or both; as un+man+ly, in which un is the prefix, ly the suffix, and man the primitive or root word.

5. — A compound word is one composed of two simple words. A hyphen is placed between the parts of a compound word. The sign + (plus) is sometimes placed between a primitive word and its prefix or suffix.

Prefix *a* means *on* or *in*.

a+shore = ashore, and means on the shore.
a+fire = afire, and means on fire or burning.
a+ground = aground, and means on the ground ; grounded.
a+bed = abed, and means in bed.

Prefix *be* means *to make.*
Prefix *co* or *con* means *with* or *together.*

Lesson 152.

Prefixes *dis* and *un* mean *not*.

dis + loyal (a.) = disloyal, means not law-abiding.
dis + similar (a.) = dissimilar, means not similar; unlike.
dis + approve (v.) = disapprove, means to blame.
dis + hearten (v.) = dishearten, means to discourage.
un + fair (a.) = unfair, means not fair; foul.
un + true (a.) = untrue, means not true; false.
un + hitch (v.) = unhitch, means to loosen.

Prefix *mis* means *wrong* or *wrongly*.

mis + lead (v.) = mislead, means to lead wrongly.
mis + deed (n.) = misdeed, means a wrong deed or act.
mis + step (v.) or (n.) = misstep, means to step wrongly;
    a wrong step.

Lesson 153.

Prefixes *fore* and *pre* mean *before*.

fore + warn (v.) = forewarn, means to warn beforehand.
fore + runner (n.) = forerunner, means one who runs before.
fore + see (v.) = foresee, means to see ahead.
pre + fix (n.) or (v.) = pre'fix or prefix', means something
    placed before; a placing before.
pre + ordain (v.) = preordain, means to ordain beforehand.
pre + historic (n.) = prehistoric, means before authentic
    history.

Lesson 154.

Suffixes (*a*)*ble* and (*i*)*ble* mean *able, fit,* or *causing.*

honor + able (a.) = honorable, means fit to be honored; worthy of honor.

bear + able (a.) = bearable, means able to be borne; capable of being borne.

rely + able (a.) = reliable, means fit to be depended upon.

contempt + ible (a.) = contemptible, means fit for contempt; unfit for respect.

> *Note.* — No comprehensive rule can be given to designate between the use of *able* and *ible.* This must be learned by practice. In case of doubt as to which should be used, consult the dictionary. Apply this note in the following words, and observe the rule for final *e.*

distinguish—, speak—, eat—, laugh—, read—, flex—, convinc(e)—, convert—, sens(e)—, inhabit—, credit—, effervesc(e)—.

Lesson 155.

Prefixes *ar, an, ian, ary,* mean *one who, that which, relating to.*

school + ar = scho(o)lar, means one who is learned.

drunk + ard = drunkard (n.), means one who gets drunk.

planet + ary = planetary (a.), means relating to planets.

adverse + ary = advers(e)ary (n.), means one who opposes.

mahomet—, rhetoric—, bound—, mission—, logic—.

> *Note.* — Note the pronunciation of " rhetoric— " when suffix is added.

Lesson 156.

Prefix *re* means *again* or *anew*.

re + elect　　= re-elect, means to elect again.
re + conquer = reconquer, means to conquer again.

Prefix *super* means *above*.

super + human = superhuman, means above human.
super + natural = supernatural, means above the natural.

To the Pupil. — Supply the proper prefixes, combine and define.

—crown, —cŏnsider, —spĕll, —pärtner, —ēqual,
—believe, —print, —lŏck, —ēasy, —wăre.

Lesson 157.

PREFIXES IN COMMON USE.

1. *A* = on or in, as in ashore.
2. *Be* = to make or made, as in befit.
3. *Co* or *Con* = with or together, as in conjoin.
4. *Dis* = not, or away, as in dissimilar, distrust.
5. *En* or *Em* = in or on, as entrap, embody.
6. *Fore, Pre* = before, as in foreclose, preordain.
7. *Mis* = wrong or wrongly, as in misspell.
8. *Re* = again, as in remember, reconsider.
9. *Super* = above, as in superhuman.
10. *Un* = not, as in unsafe, means not safe.

Lesson 158.

Suffix *dom* means *condition* or *possession*.

king + dom (n.) = kingdom, means a kind of government.
free + dom = freedom, means liberty.

Prefix *en* means, (1) in verb, *to make;* (2) in adjectives, *made.*

short + en = shorten (v.), means to make shorter.
deep + en = deepen (v.), means to make deeper.

Suffix *er* means, (1) in nouns, *one who;* (2) in adjectives, *more.*

read + er = reader (n.), means one who reads.
profound + er = profounder (a.), means more profound.

Lesson 159.

full means full of, marked by, as in fearful, joyful.
fy, ify means to make, as in justify.
hood means condition of being, as priesthood.
ion means act or state of being, as in oppression.
ize means to make; avilize; equalize.
kin, let, ling mean little, diminutive; streamlet.
ly means like, as in bravely, motherly.
ment, ness means state of being.
ous, ship, y mean state or condition of being.

Lesson 160.

Rule 13. — *Final e of a primitive word is dropped when a suffix is added that begins with a vowel.*

mănage + er = manager (n.), means one who manages.

manage + ing = managing (pres. p.), means continuing to manage.

manage + ed = managed (p.p.), means that has been managed.

ĕrāse + able = erasable (a.), means that can be erased.

erase + er = eraser (n.), means one who erases; that which erases.

erase + ing = erasing (pres. p.), means act of rubbing out.

erase + ed = erased (p.p.), means that has been rubbed out.

Note. — Treat the following words as above.

advise + able, er, ing, ed. | move + able, er, ing, ed.
value + able, er, ing, ed. | note + able, er, ing, ed.

Lesson 161.

Note. — Treat as above.

achieve + able, er, ing, ed. | excuse + able, er, ing, ed.
deşire + able, er, ing, ed. | sail + able, er, ing, ed.
cŭre + able, er, ing, ed. | guide + able, er, ing, ed.

Lesson 162.

EXCEPTIONS TO RULE 13.

EXCEPTION 1. — Words that end in *ce* or *ge* retain the final *e* on adding the suffix *able* or *ous* to keep *c* and *g* soft.

change + able = changeable.	charge + able = chargeable.
notice + able = noticeable.	storage + able = storageable.
peace + able = peaceable.	outrage + ous = outrageous.
service + able = serviceable.	courage + ous = courageous.
mortgage + able = mortgage-able.	advantage + ous = advan-tageous.

To the Pupil. — What root words in this lesson may be used both as nouns and verbs?

Lesson 163.

EXCEPTION 2. — Words that end in *oe* or *ee* retain the final *e* unless the suffix begins with *e*.

hoe + ing = hoeing.	see + ing = seeing.
toe + ing = ———	agree + ing = agreeing.
shoe + ing = ———	free + ing = freeing.

EXCEPTION 3. — A few words retain *e* to preserve their identity.

singe + ing = singeing.	twinge + ing = twingeing.
hinge + ing = hingeing.	fringe + ing = fringeing.

Lesson 164.

Rule 14. — *Final y of a primitive word, when preceded by a consonant, is changed into i on the addition of a suffix, unless the suffix begins with i.*

happy + er   = happier (a.), means more happy.
happy + ly   = happily (adv.), means in a happy manner.
happy + est = happiest (a.), means the most happy.
happy + ness = happiness (n.), means state of being happy.

To the Pupil. — Treat the following words as above.

greedy + er, ly, est, ness ; busy + er, ly, est, ness.
steady + er, ly, est, ness ; lazy + er, ly, est, ness.

Lesson 165.

envy + ed, ous, es, able ; glory + fy, ous, es, ed.
victory + ous, es ; worthy + er, ness, est.
fancy + ful, er, ed, es ; friendly + er, ly, ness, est.

glorify + ing = glorifying. │ copy + ist   = copyist.
typify + ing = typifying.   │ fancy + ing = fancying.
modify + ing = modifying.   │ baby + ish = babyish.

To the Pupil. — Why not change the y to i in the last six words? Give other examples.

Lesson 166.

Rule 15. —*Monosyllables and words accented on the last syllable, when they end with a single consonant, preceded by a single vowel, or by a vowel after qu, double the final consonant upon the addition of a suffix beginning with a vowel.*

rob + er = robber (n.), means one who robs.
rob + ing = robbing (pres. p.), means the act of robbing.
rob + ed = robbed (p.p.), means having been plundered.

thin + er, est, ed.	annul + ing, ed.
glăd + en, est, er.	control + ing, ed.
equip + ing, ed.	debar + ing, ed.
refer + ing, ed.	concur + ing, ed.

To the Pupil. — Why is the final consonant not doubled in the following words?

prevail	prevailed	vigor	vigorous
conceal	concealing	parallel	parallels
goad	goaded	intrepid	intrepidity

Lesson 167.

clăn—ish	ŭnfit—ed	unfit—ing	allot—ing
răg—ed	stir—ed	stir—ing	hem—ed
forgŏt—en	occur—ed	occur—ing	blot—ed
fŏp—ish	regret—ed	regret—ing	spot—ed

Lesson 168.

To the Teacher. — Require the pupil to form a derivative word from each of the following, and tell what rule applies, or why a rule does not apply. See that the derivative is correctly spelled.

brace	+ — = ——		luxury	+ — = ——
sense	+ — = ——		çĕremony	+ — = ——
balance	+ — = ——		melody	+ — = ——
purchase	+ — = ——		fury	+ — = ——
adore	+ — = ——		study	+ — = ——

Lesson 169.

To the Teacher. — See note above.

drop	+ — = ——		enhance	+ — = ——
forget	+ — = ——		trace + able	= trac-able
sense	+ — = ——		trace + ing	= tracing
refuse'	+ — = ——		pin	+ — = ——
acquit	+ — = ——		begin	+ — = ——

Lesson 170.

— + true = ——		— + place = ——	
— + lock = ——		— + chain = ——	
— + perfect = ——		— + coil = ——	
— + human = ——		— + patient = ——	

hope + — = ——		boy	+ — = ——
man + — = ——		shame	+ — = ——

Lesson 171.

To the Pupil.—The words of this lesson are frequently mis-spelled. Can you spell them correctly?

untie	intelligent	metallic	altogether
distillery	diligently	million	always
military	excellent	mellow	hălibut
almighty	welfare	parallel	vĭllage
răillery	artillery	pillory	stŏlid

Lesson 172.

DR. BREWER'S RULE FOR *ie* OR *ei* (Rule 16).

I before *e*
Except after *c*
Or when sounded like *a*,
As in *neighbor* and *weigh*.

i before *e* (= *ie* = *e*) except after *c* (sound of *c*):

relieve	priestly	seize	reçēive
chieftain	grievous	reçeipt	çeil
tierce	piecemeal	perçeive	conçeit
fierce	shriek	deçeive	seize

Or when sounded like *a* (*ei* = *ā*):

neighbor	inveigh	reindeer	rein
weigh	deign	skein	heinous

Lesson 173.

EXCEPTIONS TO *i* BEFORE *e*.

When *ei* = *ē* (or *ĕ* or *ī*), or when *ei* = *ī:*

nēither	hĕifer	fôrfeĭt	sŏvereĭgn
wēird	heīght	fôreĭgn	sûrfeit
ēither	sleīght	counterfeĭt	fĭnancier

Lesson 174.

per, pur.

perform	permanent	pûrsue'	pûrview
peradventure	perdition	pursu'ance	purloin
persuade	perspire	purport	purple
persevere	pervade	purgative	purvẹy
perfection	perforate	purpose	pur'gatory

Lesson 175.

er AND *re.*

prŏf'fer	ĭnfer'	thŭnder	acre (aker)
grān'ger	cŏnfer'	blŭster	măs'sacre
pĭlfer	lob'ster	blĭster	lū'cre
strānger	scŏffer	psạlter	mē'diocre

Lesson 176.

cĕnter	or centre	mēager	or meagre
sāber	" sabre	thēater	" theatre
somber	" sombre	fībre	" fibre
luster	" lustre	sĕpul'cher	" sep'ulchre

Lesson 177.

The possessive singular is generally spelled by adding an apostrophe and *s* ('s); while the possessive plural is generally formed by adding the apostrophe only.

SINGULAR.	POS. SINGULAR.	SINGULAR.	POS. SINGULAR.
girl + ('s) = girl's.		dollar + ('s) = dollar's.	
Katie + ('s) = Katie's.		lady + ('s) = lady's.	
day + ('s) = day's.		boy + ('s) = boy's.	
Longfellow + ('s) = Longfellow's.		Clark & Co. + ('s) = Clark & Co.'s.	

PLURAL.	POSSESSIVE PLURAL.	USE.
girls	+ (') = girls'.	The girls' aprons are new.
days	+ (') = days'.	Ten days' work.
dollars	+ (') = dollars'.	Two dollars' worth of goods.
ladies	+ (') = ladies'.	Those ladies' hats are spoiled.
men	+ ('s) = men's.	Men's shoes.
children	+ ('s) = children's.	Children's ways.
mice	+ ('s) = mice's.	Mice's claws.

To the Pupil. — Write the possessive of *woman, women, baby, babies, fairy, fairies.*

Lesson 178.

DEFINITION. — Accent is a stress of voice placed upon a particular syllable in a word. Accent is either primary or secondary. In the word *in'complete'*, the first syllable (*in'*) has the secondary or light accent, which is marked with a light inflection mark, thus ' ; and the last syllable (*plete'*), has the primary or main accent, and is marked with a heavier inflection mark, thus /.

To the Pupil. — In the following, and in many other words, the accent is on the first syllable when the word is a noun or adjective, and on the second syllable when it is a verb.

USE.

ab'stract (n.).	An abstract of title.
ab'stract (adj.).	An abstract or vacant stare.
abstract' (v.).	You may abstract the title.
af'fix (n.).	A suffix is sometimes called an affix.
affix' (v.).	Affix the letter to the word.
con'flict (n.).	The rebellion of 1861 is called "The Conflict."
conflict' (v.).	Two ideas may conflict.
cem'ent (n.).	Cement is a kind of mortar.
cement' (v.).	Cement the cistern.
ex'tract (n.).	The extract of lemon is an acid.
extract' (v.).	Bees extract honey from flowers.

Lesson 179.

To the Pupil. — Learn to use the following words.

găl'lant (adj.), *brave.*
gallănt' (n.), *an escort.*
in'valid (n.), *a sick person.*
invălid (adv.), *of no force.*

mĭn'ute (n.), *sixty seconds.*
mīnute' (adj.), *very small.*
per'mĭt (n.), *leave; warrant.*
permit (v.), *to allow.*

Lesson 180.

rec'ord (n.), *a register.*
record' (v.), *to register.*
rĕf'ūse (n.), *worthless re-mains.*
refuṣe' (v.), *to reject.*
sûr'vey (n.), *a view taken.*
survey' (v.), *to view.*

tôr'ment (n.), *a torture.*
torment' (v.), *to torture.*
prō'test (n.), *denial.*
protĕst' (v.), *assent; to af-firm.*
Au'gust (n.), *a month.*
augŭst (v.), *grand.*

Lesson 181.

at'tribute (n.), *a quality.*
attrĭb'ute (v.), *to ascribe.*
con'fine (n.), *a boundary.*
confine' (v.), *to shut up.*
dī'gest (n.), *a body of laws.*
dĭgest' (v.), *to dissolve.*

ĭn'cense (n.), *perfume'.*
ĭncense' (v.), *to enrage.*
ĭn'lay (n.), *a piece of work.*
inlay' (v.), *to ornament.*
ob'ject (n.), *a purpose.*
object (v.), *to oppose.*

Lesson 182.

To the Pupil. — The size of the type is shown in the name. Copy the punctuation marks.

TYPE.		PUNCTUATION.
great primer	*script*	cŏm'ma . . . . . . **,**
		sĕm'icolon. . . . **;**
English	*Italic*	pē'riod . . . . . . **.**
pica	.	ĭnterroga'tion . . **?**
small-pica	**full-face**	ĕxclāma'tion . . **!**
long-prĭmer		dash . . . . . . **—**
bourgeois'[1]	CAPITALS	parenthesis . . **( )**
brĕvier		quotation . . **" "**
mĭnion	SMALL CAPS	brackets . . . . **[ ]**
nonparĕil'[2]		hyphen . . . . . **-**
ăg'ăte		câ'ret . . . . . **∧**
pearl		apŏs'trophe . . . **'**
dia'mond[3]		

Pronounced: [1] burjois. [2] nŏn-pa-rĕl'. [3] dī -a-mond or diamŭnd.

Lesson 183.

To the Pupil. — Observe the type in each line. Learn to spell all the words.

" An honest man is the noblest work of God."

"Great character is as rare a thing as great genius."

"True courage will show itself in deeds."

"Tarnish not thy good name, neither thy fortune."

Lesson 184.

1. lăx, *loose.*
   lăcks, *wants.*
2. rōte, *mere repetition.*
   wrote, *did write.*
3. slew, *did slay.*
   slue, *to turn, to turn about.*

4. choir, *a body of singers.*
   quire, *twenty-four sheets.*
5. māze, *an intricate place.*
   maize, *Indian corn.*
6. lŏck, *a fastening.*
   loch, *a lake.*

Lesson 185.

1. hīed (v.), *made haste.*
   hide (v.), *to conceal.*
2. lapse, *to fall.*
   laps, *plural of lap.*
3. ōwed, *did owe.*
   ode, *a song.*

4. māle, *masculine.*
   mail, *armor.*
5. mīght, *strength, power.*
   mite, *a small insect.*
6. vīce, *defect, fault.*
   vise, *an instrument.*

Lesson 186.

1. plate, *a dish.*
   plait, *to braid.*
2. sale, *act of selling.*
   sail, *of a ship.*
3. soared, *did soar.*
   sword, *a weapon.*

4. tăcks, *small nails.*
   tax, *an assessment.*
5. īdle, *doing nothing.*
   idol, *an image of worship.*
6. cĕllar, *a room under ground.*
   seller, *one who sells.*

To the Teacher.—Require the pupil to use these words in sentences in which their meaning shall be illustrated.

Lesson 187.

RELATING TO ARITHMETIC.

ĭn'teger	numerātion	făctor	frăctions
ĭn'tegral	ăddĭtion	ăliquot	con'crēte
fĭgures	subtrăction	mŭltiple	compŏs'ite
cīpher	mŭltiplĭcātion	rōōt	nū'merator
dĭgits	divīsion	divīsor	dĭfference

Lesson 188.

RELATING TO GEOGRAPHY.

īsland	crāter	prāirie	trŏpics
volcāno	hĕmisphere	cŏn'fluence	pōlar
rĭvulet	lŏngitude	păr'allels	īce-berg
penĭnsula	lătitude	equā'tor	tŏrrid
ō'asis	wạter-shed	cŏm'merce (n.)	merĭdians
dĕltà	pläteau'	cŏmmērce' (v.)	ē'quinŏx
	(plä-tō')		

Lesson 189.

RELATING TO GRAMMAR.

lănguage	ădjectives	anălysis	interjĕction
phrāṣe	ădverbs	măsculine	pärticiple
dīagram	sĭngular	fĕminine	cŏmplement
prōnoun	plūral	neūter	rĕlative
prĕdicate	mŏdifier	conjŭnction	objĕctive
cŏpula	sŭb'stantive	cŏn'jugate	sŭbjec'tive

Lesson 190.

RELATING TO PHYSIOLOGY.

nŏstril	vẽrtebrae	fībril	tongue
phalănges	trāchea	mŭscles	sāli'va
cärpus	ŭlna	vŏluntary	lă'rynx
mĕtacarpus	rādius	līver	ạuricle
spinal	femur	mĭneral	vĕntricles

Lesson 191.

RELATING TO OCCUPATION.

färming	ăgriculture	wēaving	tēaming
mīning	grāzing	hạuling	mẽrchandising
shoe'-making	mĭlling	rōwing	prĭnting
prēaching	fĭshing	ship-building	black-smithing
tēaching	spōrting	tĕlĕg'raphy	banking
tailoring	trăpping	stĕnŏg'raphy	butchering

Lesson 192.

RELATING TO GEOGRAPHY.

Bangor	Rome	Chili	Alleghany
Sacramento	Odessa	Venezuela	Himalaya
Dallas	Merrimac	Russia	Scandinavian
Cologne	Missouri	Portugal	Gibraltar
Versailles	Rhine	Hindoostan	Yucatan
Niăḡ'ara	Yosĕm'ītē	Cincinnïti	Yū'kŏn

Lesson 193.

MILITARY TERMS.

căptain	ămmunition	recruit	tŏmahawk
colonel	băttălion	maneūver	ärsenal
mājor	rĕgiment	campāign	rēdoubt'
sērgeant	platōōn	còmpany	breast'-work
lieutĕnant	nāval	milĭtia	bărrack

Lesson 194.

RELATING TO MEDICINE.

morphĭne	quī'nīne	glȳcerine	pŏtash
strychnĭne	ĭpecăc	păregôric	săssafras
ălcōhol	cămphor	rhubarb	ärnica
ärsenic	īodine	ammonia	särsaparĭla
laudanum	sulphur	călomel	magnēşia
chlō'roform	ōpiate	narcŏtic	ăntimony

Lesson 195.

DISEASES.

mēasles	hȳsterics	croup	pneumōnia
scrŏfula	neūralgia	palsy	dyspĕpsia
ăsthma	parălysis	scûrvy	dĭphthēria
catärrh	rheumatism	tȳphus	erysĭp'elas.
pleurisy	scarlatïna	căncer	dysentery
jäun'dice	small'pox	gout	hȳdrophō'bia

Lesson 196.

RELATING TO BOTANY.

corŏlla	sēpal	corōna	hēliotrope
cālyx	pŏllen	ōvary	zizā'nia
stāmen	stĭgma	ōvūle	fūch'sia
pĭstil	ănther	placĕnta	. hydrăngea
pĕtal	fĭlament	hȳ'acinth	dählia

Lesson 197.

NAMES OF ANIMALS.

opŏssum	zēbra	raccōōn	lĕopard
ärmadillo	porcupine	ălligator	gorĭlla
ĕlephant	jăguär'	wọlverine'	mosquito
chimpănzee	tĕrrier	rhinŏceros	bēētle
wēasel	girăffe	llàmà	phĕasănt

Note.—Spell the plurals of the words in Lesson 197.

Lesson 198.

răp, *to strike.*

wrap, *to cover.*

mōte, *a particle of matter.*

moat, *a ditch or trench.*

lāin, *p.p. of lie.*

láne, *a narrow passage.*

mēan, *contemptible.*

miēn, *appearance.*

pēal, *a loud sound.*

peel, *to pare.*

lāid, *did lay.*

lade, *to load.*

bāil, *surety.*

bale, *a quantity or package.*

wāste, *desolate.*

waist, *part of the body.*

Lesson 199.

1. troop, *a collection of people.*
   troupe, *of players.*
2. tear, *water from the eye.*
   tier, *a row.*
3. vīal, *a small bottle.*
   viol, *a musical instrument.*
4. sāilor, *a man who sails.*
   sailer, *a thing that sails.*
5. mīner, *a worker in mines.*
   minor, *one under age.*
6. brīdle, *for a horse.*
   bridal, *belonging to a bride.*

Lesson 200.

crĭcket	pūpa	shrĭmp	prạwn
ēarwig	căterpillar	crăbs	sănd'-flẹa
gnăt	lärva	crạw-fish	trīlobite
lōcust	chrȳsalis	bärnacle	cȳclŏps
grass-hopper	maggot	ōcypōdian	dăphnia

Lesson 201.

To the Pupil.—Form sentences using the following words.

famous	renowned	celebrated	notorious
frightful	terrible	fearful	awful
extravagant	lavish	profuse	prodigious
ferocious	fierce	barbarous	savage

Lesson 202.

1. rāys, *of light.*
   raise, *to lift up.*
   raze, *to pull down.*
2. purl, *the murmur of a brook.*
   pearl, *a precious substance.*
3. seen, *beheld.*
   scene, *a view.*
   seine, *a net as for fish.*
4. soul, *a spirit.*
   sole, *only, bottom of the foot.*
5. steal, *to take without right.*
   steel, *hardened iron.*
6. ton, 2000 *pounds.*
   tun, *a large cask.*
7. loan, *an amount lent.*
   lone, *without company.*

To the Pupil. — Put the right word in the right place.

1. The army will —— the fort to the ground.
   —— of light radiate from the luminous point.
   We —— that which is fallen.
2. It is useless to cast —— before swine.
3. The setting sun presents a beautiful ——.
   Have you ever —— the fisherman using the ——?
4. What will it profit a man if he gain the whole world but lose his own ——?
   The child was the —— heir to the estate.
5. The thief will —— the horse.
   —— is a most useful ——.
6. Ship the —— of butter in a ——.
7. —— me a large sum of money.
   We left the man in the —— wood.

Lesson 203.

1. pōle, *a long stick.*
   poll, *the head.*
   Pŏll, *a parrot.*
2. tēam, *a span.*
   teem, *to be full of.*
3. metal, *iron, gold, etc.*
   mettle, *spirit, courage.*
4. märshal, *an officer.*
   martial, *war-like.*
   martial (v.), *to arrange.*
5. stâir, *a flight of .steps.*
   stâre, *to gaze at.*
6. tīde, *the flow of the sea.*
   tied, *did tie.*

To the Pupil.—Put the right word in the right place.

1. If the flag is attached to a long ——, it will flutter in the breeze.

   A —— tax is a tax levied by the head.
2. The —— took charge of the prisoner.

   —— music thrills the heart of an old soldier.
3. Horses should not display too much ——.

   Machinery is manufactured largely from ——.
4. Rivers of North America —— with fish.

   See! what a fine —— of horses that man is driving.
5. "The way into my parlor is up a winding ——."

   It is ill-manners to —— at people.
6. Wait for the turn of the ——.

   The fisherman —— his boat to the shore.

Lesson 204.

1. flew, *did fly.*
   flue, *a chimney.*
2. dȳing, *expiring.*
   dyeing, *coloring.*
3. nēed, *to require.*
   knead, *to work dough.*

4. kēy, *to lock.*
   quay, *a wharf.*
5. māin, *principal.*
   mane, *of an animal.*
6. him, *a pronoun.*
   hymn, *a song.*

To the Pupil.—Put the right word in the right place.

1. A little chĭm'ney-swạl'low built its nest in the ——.
   The eagle carried the child in its talons as it ——
   away to its aerie.
2. The old year is slowly ——.
   The —— of cloth enhances its value.
3. The —— of a more substantial form of government
   was felt by our forefathers.
   The baker will —— the dough.
4. A traveler lost his —— on the ——.
5. The orator stated his —— reasons distinctly, and
   without fear of contradiction.
   The enraged lion shook his shaggy —— in defiance.
6. We requested —— to sing the Battle —— of the
   Republic.

Lesson 205.

REVIEW.

1. I heard (6–204) sing a (6–204).
2. A (4–204) to fortune is not always a key to happiness.
3. I found a (2–202), a perfect gem, the like of which I had never seen.
4. Earth, air, and sky (2–203) with beauty which we mortals do not always see.
5. We (1–202) our eyes to Heaven and behold the (1–202) of the great sun as they come to change darkness into light.
6. Time and (6–203) wait for no man.
7. A (4–202) hope sometimes keeps the (4–202, afloat. Be hopeful and persevere.
8. (7–202) what is your own, not that which is another's.
9. (7–202) and weary, he sought a quiet spot for rest and meditation.
10. Have you ever (3–202) the splendor of a mountain (3–202)?
11. Put a (6–199) on your temper before you put on a (6–199) garb.

Note. — The first figure or number in each parenthesis refers to the number of the word, and the second number is the number of the lesson in which the word to be reviewed and inserted may be found.

Lesson 206.

ar, er, or, (=ŭr).

bĕggar	wearer	dōnor	beliēver
môrtar	stăgger	dĕbtor	sûrvey̆or
călendar	cọurier	liquor	sĭmilar
jŏcular	grōcer	lănguor	vĭsitor
tūbular	lĕdger	cŏnqueror	precĕptor

Lesson 207.

able, ible.

vĭsible	tāmable	recēivable	advīsable
suitable	plạusible	crĕdĭtable	admĭssible
ēatable	pŏssible	fēasible	īrritable
flĕxible	sūlable	assāilable	diṣcẽrn'ible
lạudable	pitiable	inflămmable	accĕptable

Lesson 208.

ise, ize, yze.

ănalyze	advertiṣe'	neū'tralize	baptize'
īdolize	capsīzc	mẽr'chandise	ariṣe
ạu'thorize	căt'echise	sŏlemnize	cĭv'ilize
paralyze	sat'yrize	fẽrtilize	thēorize
crĭticise	ĕn'terprise	sy̆mpathize	·mĕmorize

Note.—Require definitions to the words of the lessons on this page.

Lesson 209.

a, e, OR *i.*

gāyety	cĕlebrate	sălary	nūtriment
vĕrify	sĕparate	vănity	sŭpplement
cĭtadel	ĕxpiate	stŭpefy	ôrnament
rărity	mălady	tĕrrify	līneament
rarefy	rĕmedy	prodigy	ĭmplement

Lesson 210.

ain, in, ine.

fămine	ĭntĕs'tine	clandĕstine	predĕs'tine
fountain	bŭlletin	mŭrrain	detĕrmine
vĭllain	jăve'lin	sănguine	ĕrmine
mŏccasin	lĭbertine	fīrkin	dŏctrine
căbin	ûrchin	chiēftain	imăgine

Lesson 211.

ary, ery, ory.

cŏntrary	sĕminary	cŭstomary	prĕsbytery
drŭdgery	tĕrritory	perfūmery	cŏmmentary
sāvory	drāpery	prŏmissory	chicānery
bĕggary	mĕrcenary	obĭtuary	mĭllinery
cĕmetery	slĭppery	compŭlsory	anniver'sary

Note. — Require definitions to the words of each lesson on this page.

Lesson 212.

1. sēam, *of a garment.*
   seem, *to appear.*
2. plāin, *simple; level ground.*
   _ plane, *a tool; level surface.*
3. pēēr, *an equal; nobleman.*
   pier, *a support.*
4. ạltar, *a place of sacrifice.*
   alter, *to change.*
5. session, *the sitting of an assembly.*
   cession, *act of giving.*
6. cŏllar, *for the neck.*
   choler, *anger.*

1. It —— ed that the —— was a very strong one.
2. Be ——, but not rude, in speech.
   —— the board until it is a ——.
   A —— may be arid, or it may be fertile.
3. There are but few men who have not their ——.
   Iron —— s strengthened the bridge.
4. That is a devoted man who kneels at yonder ——.
   If your language be incorrect, —— it.
5. The —— of land was made at the last —— of Congress.
6. Control your temper, and do not display ——.
   A —— is for the neck.

DEFINITION. — Antonyms are words having opposite meanings, as —

equal — unequal.
sitting — standing.
appear — disappear.

active — inactive.
from — to.
join — disjoin.

Lesson 213.

1. cănvas, *coarse linen cloth.*
   canvass, *to examine.*
2. gămbol, *to frolic.*
   gamble, *to play for money.*
3. barren, *unfruitful.*
   baron, *a noble.*
4. cŭrrant, *a fruit.*
   current, *of a stream.*
5. pāin, *suffering.*
   pane, *of glass.*
6. mantel, *a chimney-piece.*
   mantle, *a cloak.*

1. A tent is made of heavy ——.
   It is well to thoroughly —— a difficult question, before passing judgment upon it.
2. Never ——. A fish may —— in the water.
3. There is no one entirely —— of good deeds.
   In days of old, ——s held their sway.
4. The Gulf Stream is the largest oceanic ——.
5. —— is often a blessing in disguise.
6. Snow is winter's sable ——.

Note.—Write antonyms of the following words.

rattle	——	cheat	——
jabber	——	fraud	——
cackle	——	deceit	——

Lesson 214.

1. mănner, *form ; way.*
   manor, *a district.*
2. mĭst, *fine rain.*
   missed, *did miss.*
3. tāper, *a wax candle.*
   tāper, *to narrow to a point.*
   tāpir, *an animal.*
4. pălate, *roof of the mouth.*
   pallet, *a small bed.*
   palette, *an instrument used by an artist.*
5. prophet, *one who foretells.*
   profit, *gain.*
6. peddle, *to sell.*
   pedal, *of a piano.*

1. The parishioner's manner tended to attach him to the people of his ——.
2. Fog and —— are quite common along the Pacific coast.
3. The weird burning of the —— cast a ghostly appearance on the surroundings.
4. A —— is made by placing blankets upon the floor. A cot is not a pallet.
5. The hope of —— is a great incentive to action.

Note 1. — The pupil will form additional sentences, using words in this lesson.
Note 2. — Give antonyms to the following synonyms.

génial	——	desperate	——
warm	——	wild	——
cordial	——	daring	——
merry	——	audăcious	——
festive	——	reckless	——

Lesson 215.

1. ăccede, *to comply with.*
   exceed, *to go beyond.*
2. ăffect', *to act upon.*
   effect, *to accomplish.*
3. băllet, *a song.*
   ballot, *a voting ticket.*
4. dōse, *a quantity.*
   doze, *to drowse.*
5. dāi'ry, *a milk-house.*
   dī'ary, *a daily register.*
6. gĕsture, *an action.*
   jester, *one who jests.*

1. —— cheerfully to what is right, but oppose strenuously what is wrong.
   A good financier will not permit his expenses to —— his income.
2. A change in temperature will —— a barometer.
   Kind words have good ——.
3. Intelligence should be the qualification for the casting of a ——.
4. A —— is an unsound sleep.
5. Do not confuse the word *dairy* with the word ——. (See definition above.)

Note 1. — Give some of the different meanings and applications of the following words.

body	mind	disquietude	peace
substance	spii	anxiety	⁄ pacification
mass	soul	uneasiness	assurance
whole	individual	apprehension	calmness

Lesson 216.

REVIEW.

1. Form sentences, using the words *pier* and *peer* (Lesson 212).

   Form sentences, using the words *collar* and *choler* (Lesson 212).

   Form sentences, using the words *current* and *currant* (Lesson 213).

2. What is the meaning of the suffixes *ar, er, or ?*

3. Analyze the words *debtor, courier, tubular.*

4. Define *mist* and *missed.*   Form sentences using these words.

5. Define suffix.   Define prefix.

6. Define synonyms ; antonyms.

7. What does *able* mean ?   Illustrate.

8. Define *need* and *knead.*

9. How is the word *seine* pronounced ?

10. Form a sentence, using the word *team.*

11. What is accent ?   How is the secondary accent marked ?

12. Define the words *him* and *hymn.*

13. Give a synonym of the word *manner.*

14. Give the name of each of the following diacritical marks : ‾, ˘, ˜.

15. What is meant by the expression, *keeping a dairy ?*

16. What is meant by the expression, *keeping a diary ?*

Lesson 217.

To the Teacher.— Require the pupil to define each word.

abrĭdge	ăn'cestry	ärtery	admĭssion
ạustere'	ăl'kaline	ambrōṣia	advīser
acquīre	ăsterisk	advĕn'ture	ămicable
angĕlic	ärchitect	ăp'erture	ärmory
abŏlish	är'mistice	audā'cious	ăqueduct
diṣobẹy'	dĭscipline	dĕlicate	decī'sive

Lesson 218.

băl'ustrade	băr'rier	brunĕtte'	brĭndle
bĕverage	bĭ'sect	blăspheme'	burlĕsque
bondage	bärbăr'ic	bŏt'any	brụtally
bāsement	bărricāde'	boundary	brōkerạge
blockāde'	brĭg'and	brăndish	brībery
devĕlop	dŭngeon	delīrious	dīplo'ma

Lesson 219.

colōgne	chărity	crĭticism	capăcity
campāign	cănopy	cŏnvent	cĕssā'tion
consĭder	crȳstal	cŏnquer	creātion
carbŏnic	cûrrency	cĕnsure	crụsader
cănnibal	cŏronet	clĕrical	cer'ēbrum
delĭcious	dĭs'course	dĭligence	drăm'atist
dūteous	diăm'eter	diăgonal	dī'alogue

Lesson 220.

To the Pupil.—Use the right word in the right place.

rein.   You can —— your horse if it should ——.   rain.
lain.   He had just —— down in the narrow ——.   lane.
knight.   The —— left in the ——.   night.
heard.   I —— a —— of cattle passing by.   herd.
wait.   —— and I will tell you your ——.   weight.
seller.   The wine —— lived in a ——.   cellar.
alter.   They propose to —— the place of the ——. altar.
pale.   The —— maid brought the —— of milk.   pail.
main.   The —— beauty of the horse is his long ——. mane.
bear.   I cannot —— to go with —— hands.   bare.

Lesson 221.

climb.   In summer we will —— to a cooler ——.   clime.
flee.   Any one would —— from a ——.   flea.
flew.   The cinder —— from the open ——.   flue.
maid.   The —— —— a bad mistake.   made.
hare.   The —— has a coat of soft brown ——.   hair.
hie.   Let us —— away to the —— hills.   high.
ate.   He —— —— plums.   eight.
need.   You —— not —— the bread so much.   knead.
key.   The —— of the boat is at the ——.   quay.
haul.   We must —— the timber to build the ——. hall.

Lesson 222.

er, ir, ur, our.

cîrcuit	fĕrvor	joûrneyman	vĕrsion
vĕrnal	fûrther	cîrcumspect	nûrture
cîrcular	mĕrmaid	pērvious	fîrmament
sûrloin	gîrdle	cûrsory	adjoûrn
tĕrminate	mĕrcury	· gîrder	intĕrpret

Lesson 223.

cal, cle, kle.

pärticle	sprĭnkle	grammătical	alphabĕtical
lŏgical	īcicle	recĭp'rocal	satĭrical
whĭmsical	phȳsical	hystĕrical	recĕptacle
trăgical	frĕckle	chrŏnicle	vēhĭcle
ŏbstacle	sûrgical	numĕrical	hĭstŏr'ical

Lesson 224.

cious, tious.

rapācious	frăctious	atrōcious	inflĕctious
flagĭtious	capācious	licĕntious	tenācious
ferōcious	offĭcious	vĭcious	ambĭtious
grācious	judĭcious	suspĭcious	nutrĭtious
pernĭcious	vexātious	vivācious	ostentātious

Note. — Define the words on this page.

Lesson 225.

tīme (n.), *a period.*
thȳme (n.), *a plant.*
Vēnus (n.), *a planet.*
venous (adj.), *relating to veins.*
bōard (n.), *a plank.*
bored (v.), *did bore.*
nąughty (adj.), *ill-bred.*
knotty (adj.), *having knots.*
bĕtter (adj.), *superior.*
bettor (n.), *one who bets.*
rĭgor (n.), *severity.*
rigger (n.), *one who rigs.*

fâiry (n.), *an imaginary being.*
ferry (v.), *act of crossing a stream by ferry.*
īslet (n.), *a small island.*
eyelet (n.), *a hole for a lace.*
līar (n.), *one who tells lies.*
lyre (n.), *a musical instrument.*
pĭllar (n.), *a column.*
pĭllow (n.), *a cushion.*

Lesson 226.

more (adj.), *a greater number.*
mower (n.), *one who mows.*
prīer (n.), *one who pries.*
prior (adj.), *previous.*
sucker (n.), *a kind of fish.*
succor (n.), *aid; help.*
rădish (n.), *a vegetable.*
reddish (adj.), *partaking of red.*
căstor (n.), *the beaver.*
căster (n.), *one who casts.*

plăintiff (n.), *a party at law.*
plaintive (adj.), *mournful.*
gēnus (n.), *class.*
genius (n.), *mental gift.*
fisher (n.), *one who fishes.*
fissure (n.), *a chasm.*
populace (n.), *the people.*
populous (adj.), *full of people.*
bĕrry (n.), *a fruit.*
bury (v.), *to cover with earth.*

Lesson 227.

incite' (v.), *to stir up.*
ĭn'sight (n.), *a deep view.*
ex'tant (v.), *now existing.*
extent' (n.), *space; size.*
frē'quent (adj.), *occurring often.*
frequent' (v.), *to visit often.*

com'pact (n.), *an agreement.*
compact' (adj.), *firm; solid.*
in'crease (n.), *growth.*
increase'(v.), *to grow greater.*
su'pine (n.), *a kind of noun.*
supine' (adj.), *lying on the back.*

Lesson 228.

To the Pupil.—Insert the proper word.

incite'.
in'sight.
  The teacher should —— her pupils to take a deeper —— of their lessons.

extent'.
ex'tant.
  Peculiar ideas of the —— of the continent were —— in the time of Columbus.

com'pact
compact'.
  The judge ordered that the —— be made in one —— body.

frequent'.
fre'quent.
  To —— the place of amusement was his —— desire.

increase'.
in'crease.
  If we —— workingmen's wages, there should be a great —— in work.

su'pine.
  The —— is not recognized by all grammarians.

supine'.
  The bones of the arm are arranged so as to allow a —— position of the hand.

Lesson 229.

To the Teacher.—Require the pupil to define each word in this lesson.

ennō'ble	ĕdify	ĕmperor	evăp'orate
estăblish	ĕpicure	ĕthical	equātion
ĕd'ucate	ĕpitaph	evăc'uate	expīring
ĕbony	ĕmphasis	ejac'ulate	expănded
ĕxodus	ĕmigrant	eman'cipate	engrāver

Lesson 230.

ARITHMETIC.

recĭp'rocal	perĭm'eter	hypŏt'enuse	alter'nate
insūr'ance	trăp'ezoid	ĕvolu'tion	rădical
advalōrem	trapēz'ium	involution	diăgonal
perpendĭcular	rhombus	specĭ'fic	scalēne
expo'nent	pŏlygon	horizon'tal	equilateral

Lesson 231.

(See note, Lesson 229.)

fanătic	fôrtitude	frĭvolous	fĭscal
fantăstic	frāgrancy	forbăde'	frŭstrum
factory	flŏrid	faucet	forĕjgner
fiftieth	fănciful	forfeiture	flĕxible
fortify	fer'rule (fĕrril)	funē'real	feasible
fōrgery	fĕlony	fugitive	fĕoff (fĕf)

Lesson 232.

To the Teacher.—Require the pupil to form, define, and use derivatives, using the root word and the prefixes and suffixes given below.

per, con, trans, in, re, de + *form* + ity, al, ance, ed.

EXAMPLES : con + form = conform, means ——.

form + al + ity = formality, means ——.

Lesson 233.

Facio (*Factum*), TO DO OR MAKE (Latin).
ROOTS : *fact, fect, ficient.*

bene, male, satis + *fact* + ion, or = ——.

EXAMPLE : bene + fact + ion = benefaction, means ——.

af, ef, de, in, per, im + *fect* = ——.

EXAMPLE : af + fect = affect, means ——.

ef, de, pro + *ficient* = ——.

EXAMPLE : de + ficient = deficient, means ——.

Pello (*Pulsum*), TO DRIVE (Latin).
ROOTS : *pel, puls.*

ex, im, com, re, pro, dis + *pel* = ——.

EXAMPLE : com + pel = compel, means ——.

ex, com, re, pro + *puls* + ion, sion, ory, ive = ——.

EXAMPLE : com + puls + ion = compulsion, means ——.

Lesson 234.

begin'	beginning	brag	bragging
appall	appalling	chat	chatting
admit	admittance	snap	snappish
abhor	abhorrence	thick	thickest
propel	propelling	twit	twitting

Lesson 235.

policy	policies	robbery	robberies
vacancy	vacancies	factory	factories
tendency	tendencies	century	centuries
faculty	faculties	agency	agencies
fishery	fisheries	cavity	cavities

Lesson 236.

When the singular ends in *o* preceded by a vowel, add *s* to form the plural.

studio	studios	tattoo'	tattoos
ratio	ratios	cam'eo	cameos
seraglio	seraglios	kangaroo	kangaroos
cuckoo	cuckoos	imbrogl'io	imbroglios
folio	folios	punctilio	punctilios

To the Teacher. — Require the pupil to mark the sounds of the principal vowels in these lessons; also to define the derivative words.

Lesson 237.

To the Pupil. — Do not say

amĕnable	for amēnable	bed-stĭd	for bŏd'-stĕad
ā nuther	" ănother	bĕn	" been (bĭn)
ăpparătus	" apparātus	blēv	" believe
arā'bic	" ăr'abic	biv'ouack	" bĭv'ouac (bivwack)
are'a	" ā'rea	bĭog'raphy	" bĭog'raphy
är'row	" ăr'row	blasphē'mous	" blă'splēmous
a'kurn	" ācôrn	bŭnnet	" bŏnnet
ăc'climate	" acclī'mate	bană'na	" banä'na
abstĕ'mious	" abstē'mious	bāde	" bădе
ăb'domen	" ăbdō'men	bălm	" bälm

Lesson 238.

chlō'rīde	for chlo'rĭde	eŏmmū'nist	for eŏm'munist
cĭvl	" cĭv'il	compâr'able	" cŏm'parable
kŏlūme	" cŏl'umn (colum)	cŏmprŏm'ise	" cŏm'promĭse
combăt'ant	" cŏm'batant	cŏn'dolence	" cŏndō'lence
kĕch	" cătch	kạwst	" cŏst
cär'bene	" cär'bīne	cŭl'inary	" cū'linary
kămly	" cälm'ly	convēr'sant	" cŏn'versant
kạw'fin	" eŏf'fin	cŏmplās'ance	" cŏm'plasance
kạw'fee	" cŏf'fee	kôrtesy	" coûrtesy' (kurtesy)
krĭk	" crēēk	kūpol'ō	" cū'polä

To the Pupil. — Practice these words until familiar with the proper pronunciation.

Lesson 239.

Pono (*Positum*), TO LAY, PUT, OR PLACE (Latin).
ROOTS: *pon, pose, posit.*

(See Direction, page 123.)

com, de, post, op, ex + *pon* + ent = ———.

EXAMPLE: com + pon + ent = component, means ———.

im, com, juxta, dis, pre, pro + *posit* + ion = ———.

EXAMPLE: juxta + posit + ion = juxtaposition, means ———.

Lesson 240.

Mitto OR *Missum*, TO SEND (Latin).
ROOTS: *mit, mise, miss.*

(See Direction, Lesson 232.)

ad, con, per, sub, re, inter + *mit* = ———.

EXAMPLE: ad + mit = admit, means ———.

sur, pre, pro + *mise* = ———.

EXAMPLE: pro + mise = promise, means ———.

re, inter, e, per, com, ad + *miss* + ion, ive, ile, ary.

EXAMPLES: per + miss + ion = permission, means ———.
com + miss + ary = commissary, means, ———.
miss + ion = mission, means ———.

Lesson 241.

heir'ess	hȳdrant	harăngue	hĕctic
hôr'tative	herōic	härlequin	hĭlărity
hŏbby	harmŏnic	härdïhood	hôr'ticulture
hăvoc	heīghten	hŏstile	hĕrmitage
hăggard	hīghland	härmonize	hạlibut

Lesson 242.

machï'nist	surgeon	instrŭctor	hŏstler
mechănic	politĭcian	apŏth'ecary	hŭckster
plăsterer	attorney	photŏg'rapher	cărrier
dāiry-man	shepherd	uphōlsterer	book-bīnder
physician	solĭcitor	compŏsitor	cobbler

Lesson 243.

ịnflāme	īvory	indôr'ser	ĭgnorāmus
invĕnt	ĭssuance	itĭnerant	īsotherm
intrinsic	ĭm'agery	ĭtal'ic	ĭm'becile
impŏs'tor	ĭn'digo	ĭn'terlude	illus'trate
ĭm'pùlse	in'stigate	ĭrrătional	ĭgnīt'able

Lesson 244.

etymology	păradigm	exclămatory	mĕtaphor
ạuxiliary	synŏpsis	subôrdinate	sĭmile
plēonasm	păragraph	supĕrlative	trănsitive
sȳnthesis	descrĭptive	subjŭnctive	declĕnsion
ellĭpsis	declărative	cŏpulative	modificātion

Lesson 245.

Corpus (*Corporis*), THE BODY (Latin).

ROOT: *corpor* (*corpus*, THROUGH *corpulentus*, FLESHY).

(See Direction, page 123.)

in + *corpor* + al, ate, ion, cle.

EXAMPLE: corpus + cle = corpuscle, means ———.

Doceo (*doctum*), TO TEACH (Latin).
ROOTS: *doc, doct.*

doc + ile, ty.

EXAMPLE: doc + ile = ———, means ———.

doct + or (n.), ine, al.

EXAMPLE: doct + (r)in(e) + al = ———, means ———.

Fluo (*fluxum*), TO FLOW (Latin).
ROOTS: *flu, flux.*

af, con, super + *flu* + ency, id, ent, ence, ous.

EXAMPLES: con + flu + ence = ———, means ———.

in + *flux* = ———, means ———.

Pel'lo (*pulsum*), TO DRIVE (Latin).
ROOTS: *pel* AND *puls.*

com, im, ex, re, pro, dis + *pel* = ———.

ANALYZE: compulsion, expulsion, repulsive, impulsive, compulsory.

Lesson 246.

Moneo (*Motum*), TO MOVE (Latin).

(See Direction, Lesson 232.)

re + *move* + able, ment.

EXAMPLE : re + move = remove, means ——.

e, com, pro + *mot* + ion, ive.

EXAMPLE : e + mot + ion = emotion, means ——.

Lesson 247.

Pes (*pedus*), A FOOT (Latin).
ROOT : *ped.*

bi, quadru, ex, im + *ped* + al, er, ite, ion, (i)ment.

EXAMPLE : ex + ped + ite = ——, means ——.

Eo (*itum*), TO GO (Latin).
ROOT : *it.*

amb, in, sed, trans + *it* + ion, al, ete, ory.

EXAMPLE : in + it + (i)al = ——, means ——.

Curro (*cursum*), TO RUN (Latin).
ROOTS : *curr, curs.*

curr + ent, ency, ex, in, pre + *curs* + ion, or, ory.

EXAMPLE : pre + curs + ory = ——, means ——.

Lesson 248.

PRONOUNCED.

dā'ta	not	dạtā	dĭlăp'idate	not	dīlăpidate
dĕc'ade	"	dē'cade	dĭmĕn'sion	"	dīmĕn'sion
decrĕp'it	"	decrĕpid	disặrm'	"	disarm'
dĕf'icĭt	"	defĭç'it	disặster	"	disăs'ter
dĭrĕct'	"	dīrĕct'	diş'dain	"	disdain'
dĭplom'a	"	dĭplōm'a	dĭvest'	"	dīvest
dĕsignāte	"	dĕz'ignate	dŏg	"	dạwg
dĕs'picable	"	despĭc'able	dōmāin'	"	dō'main
dĭdăc'tic	"	dīdăc'tic	dĭs'putant	"	dĭspū'tant
dĭgrĕs'sion	"	dīgrĕs'sion	dŭc'at	"	dūcat

Lesson 249.

enĕr'vāte	not	ĕn'ervate	fāv'orĭte	not	fāv'orīte
ĕn'gĭne	"	enjĭne'	fĕmin'ĭne	"	feminīne
ĕngrōss'	"	engrŏss'	flŏr'id	"	florid
Eūropē'an	"	Eūrō'pean	forbăde'	"	forbāde'
exặlt	"	exặlt'	forget'	"	forgĭt
exăm'ple	"	exăm'ple	fĭgū're	"	fĭgŭr
exĕc'utive	"	ĕxecū'tive	frăgĭle	"	frăgĭle
extol''	"	extol'	fĕt'id	"	fēt'id
ĕx'trȧ	"	ĕx'try	fȧucet	"	făssit
ẹyrie (āiry)	"	eyrie	fĭnănce'	"	fī'nănce

Lesson 250.

1. beau, *an escort.*
   bōw, *something for shoot-
   ing arrows.*
2. yoke, *for the neck.*
   yolk, *of an egg.*
3. mēte, *to measure.*
   meat, *animal flesh.*
   meet, *to come together.*
4. bough, *branch of a
   tree.*
   bow, *to bend.*
5. please, *to gratify.*
   plēas, *excuses, appeals.*
6. toled, *allured.*
   told, *did tell.*
   tolled, *did toll.*

1. A gallant —— will protect the lady he escorts.
   The gentleman received the —— with a bow.
2. The ox toils under a ——.
   The —— was larger than I had supposed it to be.
3. Be polite to all you ——.
   It is sometimes better to show mercy than to ——
   out justice to the offender.
   —— is not always a healthy diet.
4. A polite —— is easily made, and may as easily
   make a friend.
   The —— of the mistletoe is emblematic.
5. The attorney's —— for the criminal were very just.
   It is proper to make due effort to —— our friends.
6. The bells all ——, and we were —— the President
   was dead.
   Many a bird has been —— into a trap.

Lesson 251.

1. hĭst, *hush!*
   hissed, *did hiss.*
2. faun, *a sylvan god.*
   fawn, *a young deer.*
3. pride, *vanity.*
   pried, *did pry.*
4. wāin, *a wagon.*
   wane, *to decrease.*
5. ădds, *joins to.*
   adz, *a tool.*
6. bad, *not good.*
   băde, *past tense of bid.*

1. The speaker was —— when he denounced his country.
   ——! hark! footsteps approach! something goes wrong.
2. Note carefully the difference in the spelling of ——, a young deer, and ——, a sylvan god.
3. "—— is the never-failing voice of fools."
   I could not respect the man after I found he had wantonly —— into my private affairs.
4. Did you ever help to load the harvest —— with the golden wheat?
   Our love for the right should never ——.
5. An —— is a tool used in carpentry.
   The teacher —— more accurately than the student.
6. A —— man will do harm in the world instead of good.
   An obedient child will do as it is ——.

For a Spelling-Match.

Lesson 252.	Lesson 253.	Lesson 254.
spĕcify	rē'quiem	ĭn'teresting
sĭgnify	recur'rence	ĭmpotent
sănguinary	dĭstinguish	ĭmpĕr'il
sĕcretary	discrimina'tion	inŭn'date
sĕminary	dĕnsity	ĭrrep'arable
sătisfactory	dĕnizen	ĭrrŏv'ocable
satīety	dĕspotism	ĭndĭs'soluble
society	dĕmocrat	inex'orable
sōbriety	dĕv'astate	incx'plicable
stĭmulant	dŏctrine	improvise'
sĕttlement	dŏgmat'ical	ĭr'rigate
sĕmblance	locălity	mĭn'iature
stĕncil	lĭquidate	mūleteēr'
strătagem	loquăçity	mausolē'um
strătegy	legălity	mĭs'tletoe
sphĭnx	lĭterature	mystical
sŭspension	lĕg'islature	măearō'ni
rescĭnd	logĭ'cian	mēēr'schaum
restaurant	lī'beler	măr'riage
reconnoiter	laughable	mŏe'easin
rĕticence	lĕgible	mȳstify
rhăpsody	lēnient	māin'tenance
rĕferee'	liehen	mĕrmaid
rĕcommend'	lūdicrous	mĕdley
recu'perate	lăm'entable	mănufăc'ture

For a Spelling-Match.

Lesson 255.	Lesson 256.	Lesson 257.
refūṣal	transfīg'ure	ĕl'igible
rōsplen'dent	transatlăn'tic	elu'cidate
redŭn'dant	tranṣfūs'ible	ellĭp'tical
recēiver	trăn'sitory	embĕllish
rĕg'icide	pûrsū'ant	em'bryo
rĭg'orous	peru̱'ṣal	enăm'or
rĕc'ompense	promō'tive	enrōll'ment
rā'diance	pŭn'ishment	ē'quipoiṣe
retăl'iate	păn'tomime	equiv'alence
rapăç'ity	pătronize	errătic
rā'diator	păr'allax	exăg'gerate
resŭscitate	păr'aphrase	ĕx'cellence
revĕr'berate	pĕriġee	ĕxplĭc'it
reăn'imate	procrăs'tinate	ĕx'tirpate
recūṣ'ant	prevăr'icate	ĕxtĕn'sion
tȳp'ify	plĕas'urable	dimen'sion
tolerā'tion	prĕparā'tion	differĕn'tial
trĕpida'tion	mī'gratory	dĭscern'ment
tĕstā'tion	nŭllify	dĭsconcert'
tĕm'perature	neū'tralize	dĭscoun'tenance
trĕas'urership	noctur'nal	dominēer'ing
tȳr'anny	nōtorī'ety	duplĭc'ity
trănsgrĕssion	na̱u'tical	dŭl'cet
tormĕn'tor	necĕs'sity	dĭsso'ciate
trănscĕnd'ent	na̱u'seous	blāme'less

FOR A SPELLING-MATCH.

Lesson 258.	Lesson 259.	Lesson 260.
băffle	çĕl'lular	ēa'şel
băg'gage	çŏm'etery	ĕbulli'tion (act of boiling)
bāiliff	çĕn'tenary	ebōli'tion (breathing out)
băl'derdash	çentrĭp'etal	ecċentrĭc'ity
bāleăr'ic	çĕph'alopŏd	eċelūsiăs'tical
bălloon'	çertĭf'icate	ēelĭpse'
bandā'la	chagrĭn'	eċlogue (ĕk'log)
bechănce'	chăl'lenge	čce'stasy
befạll'	ċhamē'leon	čce'tӯpc
begĭnning	chăn'cellor	edĕn'tate
bīĕn'nial	chūnge'able	ĕd'ible
bilăt'eral	chärgc'able	ĕd'ifice
bissĕx'tile	chiēf'tain	effĭç'iency
bĭtu'minous	chinchĭl'la	effrónt'ery
blā'tant	Chineşe'	ĕfflores'çençc
blūe'bottle	ċhĭrŏg'raphy	Egӯp'tian
bōaconstrĭct'or	ċhĭrûr'gery	eī'der-down
bŏb'bin	çĭnchō'na	eighteen'
bōl'ster	çĭnerā'tion	elăpsc'
bómb (bum)	çĭn'nabar	eleċtrĭç'ity
bómbard' (v.)	çĭr'cle	elĕe'trotӯpc
bómbăs'tic	ċlăss'ical	ellĭp'soid
bōŏm'erăng	ċlăss'mate	elӯş'ium (ell'zhum)
bōwie-knife	ċlăv'icle	ĕl'zevir
bōw'man	ċlĕanşe'	emăç'erate

For a Spelling-Match.

Lesson 261.	Lesson 262.	Lesson 263.
hē'liotrope	obē'dience	nāme'sake
hĕm'orrhage	ŏb'elisk	năr'rowness
hĕp'tagon	ŏbjûr'gate	no'tional
herĕd'itary	ŏb'ligatory	nạu'seate
hĕr'esy	oblī'gingly	nạu'tilŭs
hermet'ically	oblïque' (oblēēk)	neçĕs'sitate
hĕr'ring	oblŏe'utor	neerŏp'olis
hespĕr'ides	ŏb'ōr'ate	nĕe'tar
Hĕs'sian	ŏb'sequy	neūrăl'gia
hĕş'itancy	obşĕr'vant	nĭehe (nĭck)
hexăm'eter	ŏb'stinācy	nĭg'gard
hī'bernate	obtūse'	nī'hĭlişm
hĭe'eough (kup)	oe'eupīer	nomăd'ic
hĭd'den	ŏe'eupy	nōmeneela'ture
hĭeroglỹph'ic	oe'tăg'onal	nŏn'sense
hīre'ling	ŏe'ulist	nō'tice
hŏb'ble	ū'dorant	nū'eleŭs
hōe'cake	ōdorĭf'erous	wēarisome
Hŏl'land	offĕnse'	jĕop'ardy
hŏm'age	olỹmp'iad	jŏs'tle (josle)
hōme-made	ŏm'inous	jū'bilant
hŏm'icide	• omnĭs'cient	jū'gular
hŏm'onym	ŏnerary	jūdĭç'iary
hōmŏl'ogous	op'erate	jŭnct'ure
hŏm'ot ¯pe	oppōs'able	zĕal'ot

Lesson 264.

A LESSON ON SYNONYMS.

thicken, solidify, condense, becloud, befoul.
obscure, commingle, amalgamate.
enlarge, extend, expand, coagulate.

Clouds ——. Water will —— and steam ——. Metals ——. Iron will ——, and in that way it will enlarge and become thicker, and when people commingle, or assemble in a crowd, they thicken in the sense of becoming more numerous in one locality.

Direction. — Let the pupil give other words, examples, and illustrations.

Lesson 265.

A LESSON ON SYNONYMS.

turn (verb), to spin round, deflect, revolve, rotate, deviate, incline, convert, metamorphose, change.

turn (noun), a bend, deflection, curve, deed, gift, tendency, fashion, revolution.

Turn, ——, ——, or —— the wheel. Do not —— from the path of right. We —— iron into steel. In traveling, we often come to a ——, ——, or —— in the road. One may be of a sober turn of mind, may have a gift for, or tendency toward, mathematics.

Lesson 266.

To the Pupil.—Do not say

dĕb'uty	for dĕp'uty		lâf	for läugh
dŏmiçīle	" dŏm'icĭle		lânch	" läunch
dŭn'key	" dŏn'key		lĕn'ient	" lē'nient
dramăt'ist	" drăm'atist		săssy	" sạucy
dē'strict	" dĭs'trict		săs'sage	" sạusage
ĕnjīne	" ĕn'gĭne		rē'cess	" recĕss'
fur	" fär		repâr'able	" rĕp'arable
fē'tid	" ˋfĕt'id		precĕd'ence	" precēd'ence
hostīle	" hŏs'tĭle		pīzen	" poiṣon
hydropăth'y	" hydrŏp'athy		ordē'al	" ôr'deal
ŏm'age	" hŏm'age		ŏp'ponent	" oppō'nent

Give diacritical marking, the accent, correctly pronounce and define:

Lesson 267.	**Lesson 268.**	**Lesson 269.**
railery	vehemence	tyrannic
rational	vaccinate	transparent
parent	versatile	Uranus
patriotic	vineyard	homestead
narrate	suffice	chocolate
monad	sudden	clapboard
mustache	tableau	pumpkin
robust	toward	contumely
romance	yesterday	different
piano	stamp	disfranchise

Lesson 270.

A Lesson on Synonyms.

uncover, reveal, divest, strip, lay bare.

We —— or —— a tree of its leaves. Facts are ——ed to the understanding.

expand	unfold	scrutinize	inspect
develop	spread	investigate	overhaul
enlarge	examine	search	explore

We scrutinize that which we question, and investigate that which we do not understand.

To the Teacher.— Let the pupil give the difference between "overhaul" and "explore"; between "search" and "inspect."

Lesson 271.

Synonyms.	Antonyms.	Synonyms.	Antonyms.
certain	uncertain	familiar	unaccustomed
true	untrue	common	rare
sure	doubtful	intimate	unfamiliar
unfailing	failing	new	old
positive	hesitatingly	well-acquainted	unacquainted
assured	questionable	ordinary	inordinary
defective	correct	open	closed
imperfect	perfect	accessible	barred
deficient	ample	public	private
incomplete	complete	unreserved	reserved

Lesson 272.

To the Pupil.—Learn to spell and use the following words.

1. adhērence (v.), *a cling-ing to.*
   adherents (n.), *those who cling to.*
2. assĭstance (n.), *help.*
   assistants (n.), *helpers.*
3. advīṣe' (v.), *to give coun-sel.*
   advice (n.), *counsel.*
4. attĕn'dançe (n.), *pres-ence.*
   attendants (n.), *those who attend.*
5. invāde (v.), *to enter by force.*
   invẹighed (n.), *reproved.*

6. bĕtter (adj.), *superior.*
   better (n.), *one who bets.*
7. counsel (v.), *to advise with.*
   council (n.), *a deliber-ate assembly.*
8. command (v.), *to order.*
   command (n.), *an order given.*
   commend (v.), *to praise.*
9. lĕs'son (n.), *a task.*
   lessen (v.), *to make less.*
10. way (n.), *a method; a direction.*
    wẹigh (v.), *to determine the weight.*

Lesson 273.

To the Pupil.—Do not say

căn'died	for	căn'did
sȳnod	"	sȳnod
in'trust	"	ĭn'terest
intē'gral	"	ĭn'tegral
irrātional	"	irrătional

dō'cile	for	dŏc'ile
aw'fice	"	ŏffice
mū'ṣeum	"	muṣē'um
tĕny	"	tīny
tenă'ceous	"	tēnā'cious

RULES COLLECTED.

RULE 1, p. 11. — Begin each sentence with a capital letter.

" 2, " 12. — End each question sentence with a question mark.

" 3, " 16. — Begin each proper name with a capital letter.

" 4, " 18. — Use an exclamation point (!) after an exclaiming sentence.

" 5, " 21. — Use a hyphen (-) between the parts of a compound word.

" 6, " 23. — Enclose the words of another in quotation marks (" ").

" 7, " 36. — An apostrophe (') denotes an omission or that there has been a contraction.

" 8, " 66. — All proper adjectives (words derived from proper names) should begin with capital letters.

" 9, " 68. — Most abbreviations should begin with a capital letter, and they all should be followed by a period.

" 10, " 75. — The plural of nouns ending in *y* preceded by a consonant is usually formed by changing *y* into *i* and adding *es*.

RULE 11, p. 75. — Nouns ending in *y* preceded by a vowel form their plurals in the usual way, by adding *s* to the singular.

" 12, " 76. — The plural of most nouns ending in *f* or *fe* is formed by changing *f* into *v* and adding *es*.

" 13, " 89. — Final *e* of a primitive word is dropped when a suffix is added that begins with a vowel.

EXCEPTIONS TO RULE 13 (see p. 90).

Exception 1. — Words that end in *ce* or *ge* retain the *e* on adding the suffix *able* or *ous*, to keep *c* and *g* soft.

" 2. — Words that end in *oe* and *ee* retain the final *e* unless the suffix begins with *e*.

" 3. — A few words retain final *e* to preserve their identity.

RULE 14, p. 91. — Final *y* of a primitive word, when preceded by a consonant, is changed into *i* on the addition of a suffix, unless the suffix begins with *i*.

" 15, " 92. — Monosyllables and words accented on the last syllable, when they end with a single consonant preceded by a single vowel, or by a vowel after *qu*, double the final consonant upon the addition of a suffix beginning with a vowel.

English Language.

Hyde's Lessons in English, Book I. For the lower grades. Contains exercises for reproduction, picture lessons, letter writing, *uses* of parts of speech, etc. . . . . $ .35

Hyde's Lessons in English, Book II. For Grammar schools. Has enough technical grammar for correct use of language . .50

Hyde's Lessons in English, Book II. with Supplement. Has in addition to the above, 118 pages of technical grammar . .60
Supplement bound alone 30

Hyde's Derivation of Words 15

Mathew's English Grammar with Selections 70

Buckbee's Primary Word Book 25

Badlam's Suggestive Lessons in Language. Being Part I. and appendix of Suggestive Lessons in Language and Reading . . .50

Smith's Studies in Nature, and Language Lessons. A combination of object lessons with language work .50 Part I bound separately 25

Meiklejohn's English Language. Treats salient features with a master's skill and with the utmost clearness and simplicity . . 1.20

Meiklejohn's English Grammar. Also composition, versification, paraphrasing, etc. For high schools and colleges 80

Meiklejohn's History of the English Language. 78 pages. Part III. of English Language, above 30

Williams' Composition and Rhetoric by Practice. For high school and college. Combines the smallest amount of theory with an abundance of practice. Revised edition. 90

Strang's Exercises in English. Examples in Syntax, Accidence, and Style for criticism and correction. Revised edition . . .45

Hempl's Old English Grammar and Reader 25

Huffcutt's English in the Preparatory School. Presents as practically as possible some of the advanced methods of teaching English grammar and composition in the secondary schools . . .25

Woodward's Study of English. Discusses English teaching from primary school to high collegiate work 25

Genung's Study of Rhetoric. Shows the most practical discipline of students for the making of literature 25

In addition to the above we have text-books in English and American Literature, and many texts edited for use in English Literature classes.

D. C. HEATH & CO., PUBLISHERS.
BOSTON, NEW YORK & CHICAGO.

READING.

Wright's Nature Readers: Sea-side and Way-side.

Boards. Illustrated. No. I., 95 pages. Price, 25 cents. No. II., 184 pages. Price, 35 cents. No. III., 300 pages. Price, 50 cents. No. IV., 000 pages. Price, 60 cents.

Designed for schools and families. Intended to awaken in children a taste for scientific study, to develop their powers of attention, and to encourage observation, by directing their minds to the living things that meet their eyes on the road-side, at the sea-shore, and about their homes.

The First Reader treats of crabs, wasps, spiders, bees, and some mollusks. The Second Reader treats of ants, flies, earth-worms, beetles, barnacles, star-fish, and dragon-flies. The Third Reader has lessons in plant life, grasshoppers, butterflies, and birds. The Fourth Reader treats of world life in its different aspects and periods.

Badlam's Suggestive Lessons in Language and

Reading. A Manual for Primary Teachers. Cloth, square. 283 pages. Price, $1.50.

A thoroughly helpful book, the outgrowth of a real experience, and of such a suggestive character that its lessons cannot fail in their adaptability to the various grades.

The first part gives *Outline Lessons for Oral Work*, specimens of stories told by children, and simple fables for reproduction.

The second part is devoted to *Suggestive Lessons* for blackboard reading and word-building. The plan embraces the best known features of the various methods of teaching.

Badlam's Primer. In the series "Stepping Stones to Reading."

Illustrated. Boards. 131 pages. Price, 25 cents.

Its main features are its simplicity, variety, and gradual development of the lessons.

Badlam's First Reader. Illustrated. Boards. 170 pages. Price, 30 cts.

Follows and develops the general plan of the Primer.

Fuller's Illustrated Primer. Illustrated. Boards. 103 pages. 25 cts.

This book presents the "Word Method" in an attractive form for little children.

Fuller's Phonic Drill Charts.

Three Charts. Manilla paper. 30 x 42 inches. Price, unmounte¹, $1.25; mounted, $2.25.

These charts have been prepared for the purpose of exercising pupils in making the elementary sounds and in combining these to form syllables and words

Smith's Reading and Speaking. Familiar Talks to Young Men

who would Speak well in Public. Cloth. 171 pages. Price, 60 cents.

A collection of suggestions to would-be speakers, consisting of informal talks on matters of importance to all young men.

Readers for Home and School.

A series of volumes to be edited by Professor CHARLES ELIOT NORTON, of Harvard University, and Miss KATE STEPHENS.

This series is to be of material from the standard imaginative literature of the English language. It will draw freely upon the treasury of favorite stories, poems, and songs with which every child should become familiar, and which have done most to stimulate the fancy and direct the sentiment of the best men and women of the English-speaking race.

[In preparation.

D. C. HEATH & CO., Publishers, Boston, New York, Chicago, and London.

MUSIC. ❋ ❋ ❋

Those desiring to introduce or change Music in their schools will find it to their interest to examine Whiting's **PUBLIC SCEOOL MUSIC SERIES.**   It contains :

1. **The Graded School Series,** Five Books, each 25 cents.
2. **The High School Music Reader,** 54 cents.
3. **The Complete Music Reader,** 75 cents.
4. **The Part-Song and Chorus Book** (for advanced classes), 96 cents.
5. **The Music Charts** (First Series, $6.00; Second Series, $3.00).
6. **Music Leaflets** (Popular Songs, Exercises, etc.), 3 cents up.

FOR UNGRADED AND COUNTRY SCHOOLS:—

7. **The Young People's Song Book,** 35 cents.

The features which commend this series of books to teachers and pupils are : Careful Grading ; Beautiful and Appropriate Illustrations ; the Latest and most Helpful Devices ; The Variety and Excellence of the Selections from the best German, English and French Composers ; and the economy in prices.

❋ ❋ ❋ DRAWING.

The remarkable success of the **THOMPSON DRAWING SERIES** and the hearty praise it is receiving from those using it, justify us in calling attention to the following features :

1. **The Primary Free-Hand Series,** Four Books, per doz., $1.00.
2. **The Advanced Free-Hand Series,** Four Books, per doz., $1.50.
3. **The Model and Object Series,** Three Books, per doz., $1.75.
4. **The Æsthetic Series,** Six Books, per doz., $1.50.
5. **The Manual Training Guides,** Two Books, each 25 cents.
6. **The Mechanical Series,** Six Books (*in press*).
7. **The Teacher's Manuals** (the most complete and helpful guides for teachers published : Primary Free-Hand Manual, 40 cents; M. and O. Manual, 35 cents; the Æsthetic Manual, 60 cents; Mechanical Manual, *in press*).
8. **The Thompson Models.**

Suggestive courses for schools furnished on application.

For other information, sample pages, etc., address,

D. C. HEATH & CO.,
BOSTON, NEW YORK, CHICAGO, LONDON.

Educational and Industrial Drawing.

By LANGDON S. THOMPSON, A. M., recently Professor of Drawing in Purdue University and now Supervisor of Drawing in the Schools of Jersey City, N. J.

THIS system of drawing is accompanied with an abundant supply of apparatus. The author has had many years experience in teaching from the lowest Primary through the Grammar, High and Technical School, and it is believed that his books are so well thought out, philosophically and practically, as to adapt themselves to all approved methods and views in the study of drawing.

The entire System will consist of the following:

1. Manual Training Series; Two Manuals. *Ready.* 25 cts. each.
2. Primary Freehand Series; Four Drawing Books and Manual. *Ready.* $1 per doz.
3. Advanced Freehand Series; Four Drawing Books *Ready.* $1.50 per doz.

The remaining Series are in preparation.

4. Model and Object Series; Three Drawing Books and Manual.
5. Historical Ornament Series; Three Drawing Books and Manual.
6. Decorative Design Series; Three Drawing Books and Manual.
7. Geometrical Series; Two Drawing Books and Manual.
8. Orthographic Projection Series; Two Drawing Books and Manual.
9. Perspective Series; Three Drawing Books and Manual.

16 wooden models, with sticks in 3 lengths and tin forms, have been prepared to accompany the above. Complete, in box, price,

Each of the **Manual Training** Books contains about 60 large pages of printed matter profusely illustrated with diagrams: No. 1 treats of Clay Modelling; Stick and Tablet Laying; Paper Folding and Cutting; Color; and the construction of Geometric Solids. No. 2 treats of Mechanical Drawing; Clay Modelling in relief; Color; Wood Carving; Paper Cutting and Pasting.

The Primary Freehand Series are each $7\frac{1}{2}$ x $9\frac{1}{2}$ inches in size. They contain carefully graded methods of work that may be used separately or simultaneously at the choice of the teacher: viz. Drawing from Copy, Drawing from Dictation, Drawing from Memory, Inventive Drawing, Supplementary Lessons on Common Objects, Drill Exercises for Free Movements and Drawing from Imagination. All the methods of work are fully explained in the **Primary Freehand Manual.** (30 cents.)

The Advanced Freehand Series are each 9 x 12 inches in size. They treat of the principles of pottery design and the conventionalization of plant forms for purposes of design.

SCIENCE.

Organic Chemistry : An Introduction to the Study of the Compounds of Carbon.

By IRA REMSEN, Professor of Chemistry, Johns Hopkins University, Baltimore. 374 pages. Cloth. Price by mail, $1.30; Introduction price, $1.20.

The Elements of Inorganic Chemistry : Descriptive and Qualitative.

By JAMES H. SHEPARD, Professor of Chemistry in So. Dakota. Agricultural Col. 399 pages. Cloth. Price by mail, $1.25 ; Introduction price, $1.12.

The Elements of Chemistry : Descriptive and Qualitative. Briefer Course.

By JAMES H. SHEPARD, Professor of Chemistry in So. Dakota Agricultural College. 248 pages. Price by mail, 90 cts.; Introduction price, 80 cts.

Elementary Practical Physics. Or Guide for the Physical Laboratory.

By H. N. CHUTE, Instructor in Physics, Ann Arbor High School, Mich. Cloth. 407 pages. Price by mail, $1.25 ; Introduction price, $1.12.

The Laboratory Note-Book. For Students using any Chemistry.

Giving printed forms for "taking notes" and working out formulæ. Board covers. Cloth back. 192 pages. Price by mail, 40 cts.; Introduction price, 35 cts.

The Elements of Chemical Arithmetic : With a Short System of El

ementary Qualitative Analysis. By J. MILNOR COIT, M. A., Ph. D., Instructor in Chemistry, St. Paul's School, Concord, N. H. 93 pp. By mail, 55 cts. ; Introduction price, 50 cts.

Chemical Problems. Adapted to High Schools and Colleges.

By JOSEPH P. GRABFIELD and T. S. BURNS, Instructors in General Chemistry in the Mass. Inst. of Technology. Cloth. 96 pages. Price by mail, 55c. Introduction price, 50c.

Elementary Course in Practical Zoology.

By B. P. COLTON, A. M., Professor of Science, Illinois Normal University. Cloth. 196 pages. Price by mail, 85 cts. ; Introduction price, 80 cts.

First Book of Geology.

By N. S. SHALER, Professor of Palæontology, Harvard University. 272 pages, with 130 figures in the text. Price by mail, $1.10 ; Introduction price, $1.00.

The Teaching of Geology.

By N. S. SHALER, author of First Book in Geology. Paper. 74 pages. Price, 25 cents.

Modern Petrography. An Account of the Application of the Microscope to the

Study of Geology. By GEORGE HUNTINGTON WILLIAMS, of the Johns Hopkins University Paper. 35 pages. Price, 25 cents.

Astronomical Lantern and How to Find the Stars.

By REV. JAMES FREEMAN CLARKE. Intended to familiarize students with the constellations, by comparing them with fac-similes on the lantern face. Price of the Lantern, in improved form, with seventeen slides and a copy of "HOW TO FIND THE STARS," $4.50 "HOW TO FIND THE STARS," separately. Paper. 47 pages. Price 15 cts.

D. C. HEATH & CO., Publishers.

BOSTON, NEW YORK, AND CHICAGO.

GEOGRAPHY AND MAPS.

Redway's Manual of Geography.

MODERN FACTS AND ANCIENT FANCIES. Cloth. 175 pages. Price, 65 cents.

This book renders the latest discoveries in Geography available for the use of teachers. A part of the work is devoted to the discussion of old traditions that still cumber many text-books. It is full of useful hints, and of bright, interesting information.

Redway's Reproduction of Geographical Forms.

I. SAND AND CLAY MODELING. II. MAP-DRAWING AND MAP-PROJECTION. Illustrated. Paper. 84 pages. Price, 30 cents.

Nichols' Topics in Geography.

Cloth. 176 pages. Price, 65 cents.

Contains a comprehensive outline of all geographical facts usually taught in our best primary and grammar schools, together with many excellent suggestions for increasing the interest of pupils, and much information of interest not usually accessible to teachers.

Jackson's Earth in Space, or Astronomical Geography.

Illustrated. Cloth. 80 pages. Price, 40 cents.

Presents, in a few simple lessons, the main facts of this world's relation to other worlds.

Picturesque Geography.

Twelve plates, 15 x 20 inches, and descriptive pamphlet. Per set, $3.00; mounted, $5.00.

Intended to picture the natural divisions of land and water, and at the same time to meet the modern demand for artistic and instructive pictures for decoration of schoolrooms.

Progressive Outline Maps :

United States, United States, No. 2 (with State boundaries), World on Mercator's Projection * (12 x 20 in.); North America, South America, Europe, Central and Western Europe,* Africa, Asia, Asia Minor, Australia, British Isles,* England,* Greece,* Italy,* Palestine.* New England, Middle Atlantic States, Southern States, Southern States — western section, Central Eastern States, Central Western States, Pacific States, New York, Ohio, Washington (State), The Great Lakes, (each 10 x 12 in.). 2 cts. each; per hundred, $1.50. Those marked with a star (*) may be had with black outline for historical study. Samples sent on receipt of 10 cents. Circulars free.

Heath's Outline Map of the United States.

Small (desk) size, 2 cts. each; $1.50 per hundred. Intermediate size, 28 x 40 inches, each 30 cts.; large size, 50 cts.; mounted, $3.00.

Roney's Student's Outline Map of England.

For use in English History and Literature, to be filled in by pupils. 5 cts.

Outline Map of Ancient History.

For recording historical growth and statistics (14 x 17 in.), 3 cts. each; per hundred, $2.50.

Practical School Maps.

Printed from entirely new plates, and including the latest geographical discoveries and political changes. Includes Europe, Asia, Africa, North America, South America, Hemispheres, United States, Palestine, and Canaan. [In press, ready soon.

D. C. HEATH & CO., Publishers, Boston, New York, Chicago, and London.

English Literature.

Hawthorne and Lemmon's American Literature. A manual for high schools and academies $1.12

Meiklejohn's History of English Language and Literature. For high schools and colleges. A compact and reliable statement of the essentials; also included in Meiklejohn's English Language (see under English Language) 80

Meiklejohn's History of English Literature. 116 pages. Part IV. of English Literature, above 40

Hodgkins' Studies in English Literature. Gives full lists of aids for laboratory method. Scott, Lamb, Wordsworth, Coleridge, Byron, Shelley, Keats, Macaulay, Dickens, Thackeray, Robert Browning, Mrs. Browning, Carlyle, George Eliot, Tennyson, Rossetti, Arnold, Ruskin, Irving, Bryant, Hawthorne, Longfellow, Emerson, Whittier, Holmes, and Lowell. A separate pamphlet on each author. Price 5 cts. each, or per hundred, $3.00; complete in cloth (adjustable file cover $1.50) 1.00

George's Wordsworth's Prelude. Annotated for high school and college. Never before published alone. 1.25

George's Selections from Wordsworth. 168 poems chosen with a view to illustrate the growth of the poet's mind and art . . 1.50

George's Wordsworth's Prefaces and Essays on Poetry . . .50

George's Webster's Speeches 1.50

George's Burke's American Orations 60

George's Webster's Speeches. *In press.*

Corson's Introduction to Browning. A guide to the study of Browning's Poetry. Also has 33 poems with notes . . . 1.50

Corson's Introduction to the Study of Shakespeare. A critical study of Shakespeare's art, with examination questions . 1.50

Corson's Introduction to the Study of Milton. *In press.*

Corson's Introduction to the Study of Chaucer. *In press.*

Hempl's Old English Grammar and Reader. 25

Cook's Judith. The Old English epic poem, with introduction, translation, glossary and fac-simile page 1.50

Cook's English Prose Style and the English Bible 50

Simonds' Sir Thomas Wyatt and his Poems. 168 pages. With biography, and critical analysis of his poems 75
[Pupils' Edition, paper, 30c.]

Hall's Béowulf. A metrical translation 1.00

Scudder's Shelley's Prometheus Unbound. With Introduction and copious Notes for students' use 60

See also our list of books for the study of the English Language.

D. C. HEATH & CO., PUBLISHERS.
BOSTON, NEW YORK & CHICAGO.

Old South Leaflets.

By special arrangement with the Directors of the Old South Studies in History and Politics, we have become the publishers for schools and the trade of the new general series of Old South Leaflets. These Leaflets are prepared by Mr. Edwin D. Mead, and are largely reproductions of important original papers, accompanied by useful historical and bibliographical notes. They consist, on an average, of sixteen pages, and are sold at the low price of five cents a copy or three dollars per hundred. The Old South work, which has been sustained in Boston for several years by Mrs. Hemenway, is a work for the education of the people, and especially the education of our young people, in American history and politics, and its promoters believe that few things can contribute better to this end than the wide circulation of such Leaflets as those now undertaken. The aim is to bring important original documents within easy reach of everybody. It is hoped that professors in our colleges and teachers everywhere will welcome them for use in their classes, and that they may meet the needs of the societies of young men and women now happily being organized in so many places for historical and political studies.

There are at present thirty-eight leaflets; others will rapidly follow. The following are the titles of those now ready:

No. 1. The Constitution of the United States. 2. The Articles of Confederation. 3. The Declaration of Independence. 4. Washington's Farewell Address. 5. Magna Charta. 6. Vane's "Healing Question." 7. Charter of Massachusetts Bay, 1629. 8. Fundamental Orders of Connecticut, 1638. 9. Franklin's Plan of Union, 1754. 10. Washington's Inaugurals. 11. Lincoln's Inaugurals and Emancipation Proclamation. 12. The Federalist, Nos. 1 and 2. 13. The Ordinance of 1787. 14. The Constitution of Ohio. 15. Washington's Circular Letter to the Governors of the States, 1783. 16. Washington's Letter to Benjamin Harrison, 1784. 17. Verrazzano's Voyage. 18. The Swiss Constitution. 19. The Bill of Rights, 1689. 20. Coronado's Letter to Mendoza, 1540. 21. Eliot's Narrative, 1670. 22. Wheelock's Narrative, 1762. 23. The Petition of Rights, 1628. 24. The Grand Remonstrance, 1641. 25. The Scottish National Covenant, 1638. 26. The Agreement of the People, 1648-9. 27. The Instrument of Government, 1653. 28. Cromwell's First Speech, 1653. 29. The Discovery of America, from the Life of Columbus by his son, Ferdinand Columbus. 30. Strabo's Introduction to Geography. 31. The Voyages to Vinland, from the Saga of Eric the Red. 32. Marco Polo's Account of Japan and Java. 33. Columbus's Letter to Gabriel Sanchez, describing the First Voyage and Discovery. 34. Amerigo Vespucci's Account of his First Voyage. 35. Cortes's Account of the City of Mexico. 36. The Death of De Soto, from the "Narrative of a Gentleman of Elvas." 37. Early Notices of the Voyages of the Cabots. 38. Funeral Oration on Washington.

Price, 5 cents a copy, or $3.00 per hundred. Nos. 14 and 18, 6 cents a copy, or $4.00 per hundred.